D0099191

SPLIT

IMAGE

ROBERT B. PARKER

G. P. PUTNAM'S SONS

New York

G. P. PUTNAM'S SONS
Publishers Since 1838
Published by the Penguin Group
Penguin Group (USA) Inc., 375 Hudson Street, New York,
New York 10014, USA • Penguin Group (Canada), 90 Eglinton Avenue East,
Suite 700, Toronto, Ontario M4P 2Y3, Canada (a division of
Pearson Penguin Canada Inc.) • Penguin Books Ltd, 80 Strand, London
WC2R 0RL, England • Penguin Ireland, 25 St Stephen's Green, Dublin 2,
Ireland (a division of Penguin Books Ltd) • Penguin Group (Australia),
250 Camberwell Road, Camberwell, Victoria 3124, Australia (a division of
Pearson Australia Group Pty Ltd) • Penguin Books India Pvt Ltd,
11 Community Centre, Panchsheel Park, New Delhi–110 017, India •
Penguin Group (NZ), 67 Apollo Drive, Rosedale, North Shore 0632,
New Zealand (a division of Pearson New Zealand Ltd) • Penguin Books
(South Africa) (Pty) Ltd, 24 Sturdee Avenue, Rosebank,
Johannesburg 2196, South Africa

Penguin Books Ltd, Registered Offices: 80 Strand, London WC2R 0RL, England

Library of Congress Cataloging-in-Publication Data

Parker, Robert B., date.
Split image/Robert B. Parker.
p.   cm.
ISBN 978-0-399-15623-6
1. Stone, Jesse (Fictitious character)—Fiction.   2. Police—Massachusetts—Fiction.   3. Cults—
Fiction.   4. Domestic fiction.   5. Police chiefs—Fiction.   I. Title.
PS3566.A686S67   2010   2009036346
813'.54—dc22

Printed in the United States of America
1   3   5   7   9   10   8   6   4   2

BOOK DESIGN BY AMANDA DEWEY

For Joan, of course, and also for Stephen F. O'Loughlin, Jr.

SPLIT IMAGE

M OLLY CRANE STUCK her head into the open doorway of
   Jesse's office and said, "Chief Stone, there's a private detective from Boston here to see you."

"Show him in," Jesse said.

"It's a her," Molly said.

"Even better," Jesse said.

Molly smiled and stepped aside, and Sunny Randall came
in, carrying a straw shoulder bag and wearing a green sleeveless
top with white pants and color-coordinated sneakers.

"Wow," Jesse said.

"Wow is good," Sunny said, and sat down.

"And accurate," Jesse said. "It couldn't have been easy getting into those pants."

"For whom?" Sunny said.

Jesse smiled.

"Shall I close the door?" he said.

"No," Sunny said. "I'm actually here on business."

"All work and no play," Jesse said.

"We'll address that at another time," Sunny said.

"That's encouraging," Jesse said.

"It's meant to be," Sunny said. "Do you know of a small religious organization here in Paradise called the Renewal? Or the Bond of the Renewal?"

"I'm the chief of police," Jesse said. "I know everything."

"Exactly why I'm here," Sunny said.

She smiled.

"Tell me about the Renewal," she said.

"They're located in a house near the town wharf. Nice house; one of the elders owns it. They all live there in a kind of communal way, run by a guy who calls himself the Patriarch. About forty, with gray hair, which Molly Crane claims is artificial."

"He dyes it gray?" Sunny said.

"What Molly claims," Jesse said. "There's a couple of so-called elders, 'bout your age, I would guess."

"Hey," Sunny said.

"I mean they're not very elder-ish."

"Okay," Sunny said.

"Rest of them are mostly kids," Jesse said. "All of whom, far as I can tell, are old enough to do what they want."

"What do they do?"

"They preach, they hand out flyers, they go door-to-door, raising money."

"They got some kind of special belief?"

"They're in favor of renewal," Jesse said.

"What the hell does that mean?"

Jesse grinned.

"Renewing the original intent of Christianity," Jesse said. "At least as they understand it. Love, peace, that kind of thing."

"Wow," Sunny said. "Subversive."

"You bet," Jesse said. "Town hates them, want me to chase them out of town."

"Which you haven't done."

"They haven't committed a crime," Jesse said.

"So, what's the complaint?"

"They're not one of us," Jesse said. "And they're kind of ratty-looking."

"They preach on the streets?" Sunny said.

"Yes."

"That can be annoying," Sunny said.

"It is," Jesse said. "It's annoying as hell, but it's not illegal."

"And you're hung up on the Constitution?" Sunny said.

"Old school," Jesse said.

"And the town council understands?"

"I don't believe so," Jesse said.

"And you care what the town council understands," Sunny said.

"Not very much," Jesse said.

They were quiet for a moment. The silence was comfortable.

"You want to know why I'm asking?" Sunny said, after a time.

"Yep."

"But not enough to ask," Sunny said.

"I knew you'd tell me."

2

SUITCASE SIMPSON DROVE the Paradise police car across the causeway to Paradise Neck, with the sun bouncing brightly off the open ocean to his right and the sheltered harbor to his left. He always thought the ocean reflected the sun more brightly than the harbor, but Jesse always laughed at him when he said it, so he didn't say it anymore. Still thought so, though.

He had the morning shift, seven to two on the east side of town, along the water. Arthur Angstrom was on the west side. It was noon. A Cadillac Escalade was parked at an angle on the roadside, just past the Paradise Neck end of the causeway. Simpson pulled up behind it and got out. The car was empty, and there were no keys in sight. Suit tried the door. It was unlocked. He got in and sat in the driver's seat. He opened the glove compartment. The car was registered to Petrov Ognowski. He found the button inside the glove compartment and popped the tailgate. Then he got out and took a look.

There was a dead man.

The back of his head was black with dried blood. Suit felt for a pulse in the man's neck. There was none. And his skin was cold. Suit went back to the cruiser and called it in.

"Molly? Suit. I got a stiff in the back of a Cadillac SUV, out at the Neck end of the causeway."

"You want an ambulance?" Molly said.

"Pretty sure he's dead, but no harm," Suit said. "Where's Jesse."

"He's out of the office," Molly said. "I'll send him when I find him."

"Okay."

"You know who it is?" Molly said.

"Car's registered to Petrov Ognowski," Suit said. "I don't know if the stiff is him."

"You haven't searched him," Molly said.

"No."

"Don't blame you," Molly said. "Here we all come."

The first to arrive was Arthur. He pulled his cruiser in behind Suit's and walked over and looked in the back of the SUV.

"Back of his head's all fucked up," Arthur said.

"I figure that's where he got shot," Suit said.

"Nice police work, Suit."

Simpson grinned.

"But there's no exit wound that I can see."

"So?"

6

"Just observing," Suit said.

Behind them, from the Paradise end of the causeway, there was the sound of a siren.

"You search him?" Arthur said.

"We got people to do that, don't we?"

"Sure, State ME will inventory everything."

"So why don't we let him search?" Suit said. "'Less you want to?"

"Search him?"

"Yeah."

"We can let the ME do it," Arthur said.

The siren faded as the ambulance pulled up and two EMTs got out. One was a woman. Her name was Annie Lopes.

"Whaddya got?" she said.

"Looks like a murder," Arthur said.

Suit said, "Unless he shot himself in the head and then climbed into the back and pulled the tailgate shut."

"That how you found him?" Annie said.

"Yep."

The two EMTs went and looked at the body. Annie put her hand to his throat and put her hand on his face. She picked up his right arm and let it fall.

"He's already starting into rigor," she said.

"So he is dead," Arthur said.

"Mostly they are," Annie said, "when they're in rigor."

The second EMT was a guy named Ralph.

"Find any keys?" Ralph said.

"Nope."

"How'd you open the back?" Ralph said.

"Car was unlocked," Suit said. "I popped the tailgate."

Annie laughed softly.

"Wow," she said.

"Cops have their ways," Suit said.

More sirens sounded across the causeway.

O NE MEMBER of the Renewal is a kid named Cheryl DeMarco. She just turned eighteen, and her parents want me to get her out."

"Whether she wants to get out or not?" Jesse said.

"I explained that if she didn't want to leave," Sunny said, "there wasn't a lot I could do."

"And?"

"They asked if I knew anybody who could remove her forcibly."

"Which of course you do," Jesse said.

"I told them I didn't," Sunny said.

"A white lie," Jesse said.

Sunny smiled.

"True," she said. "But I thought I'd rather not conspire in a kidnapping."

"I'll keep the parents in mind," Jesse said, "if the kid turns up missing."

"They didn't press it," Sunny said. "They asked if maybe I could find her and talk with her."

"The Renewal is not exactly secret," Jesse said. "How come they don't know where to find her?"

"I think the whole thing scares them," Sunny said.

Jesse nodded.

"Do you have any reason to think the Renewal is dangerous?" Sunny said.

"No."

"People are scared by things they don't understand," Sunny said.

"Yep."

"You know what else I think?" Sunny said.

"No," Jesse said. "I don't."

Sunny made a face at him.

"I think they're scared of the kid," she said.

"Physically?"

Sunny shook her head.

"No," she said. "I think they don't want her to be mad at them."

"I would have guessed she might be a little mad at them already," Jesse said.

"Leaving home and joining an unorthodox religious group?" Sunny said.

"Seems like there might be some sort of anger in there."

"Rebellion?" Sunny said. "Yes, I suppose. Maybe it's justified."

"Maybe it is," Jesse said.

"You're a big help."

"I try," Jesse said.

"So, where do I find this group?" Sunny said.

"Down near the Gray Gull," Jesse said. "I'll take you down."

Sunny looked at her watch.

"Good heavens, where does the time go," she said. "It's noon."

"Lunch?" Jesse said.

"It's right near the Gray Gull anyway," Sunny said.

"Sure," Jesse said.

"We can eat lunch and head over to the Renewal."

"Spike work the lunch hour?" Jesse said.

"Lunch is a little early for Spike to be up," Sunny said. "But you and I are enough."

"Funny you should show up so close to lunch," Jesse said.

"I'm a bear for timing," Sunny said. "You mind?"

"No," Jesse said. "I like it."

THEY HAD ICED TEA and lobster rolls. Jesse had french fries with his. Sunny didn't. Sitting across the table from him, Sunny studied Jesse. He was very much of a piece, she thought, like Richie. Compact, graceful, all his movements both precise and easy.

He looks so perfectly integrated, she thought.

"Anything from Jenn?" she said.

Jesse shook his head.

"We're not in touch," he said.

"She's really gone?" Sunny said.

"She's really gone," Jesse said.

"How do you feel about that?"

Jesse shook his head.

"You and Dix," he said. "We've both had too much shrinkage."

"Clever dodge," Sunny said.

Jesse nodded.

"Okay," he said. "I'll talk about it if you want. But afterwards you gotta talk about Richie."

"God, you're tough," Sunny said.

"Of course," Jesse said. "I'm the chief of police."

He ate a french fry.

"Okay," Sunny said.

Jesse nodded.

"Whaddya want to know?" he said.

"How you feel about her being gone?"

"Part of her I miss," Jesse said. "Part of her was—still is, I guess—simply sensational. Funny, charming, smart, quick, loving, sexy. It's the part of her I loved—probably still love, I guess. I'll probably always miss that."

"Of course you will," Sunny said. "Anyone would. . . ."

"But finally, I guess, it came with too much else."

"Like?"

"The desperate need to be . . . what? Important?" Jesse said. "Successful? Special?"

"The need to be noticed?" Sunny said.

"Yes," Jesse said. "It ate her up, and she couldn't seem to overcome it."

"You know why?"

"Why she needed to be noticed?" Jesse said.

"Yes."

"No."

"Does she?" Sunny said.

"I don't know," Jesse said. "She still needs it."

"And you were not enough," Sunny said.

Jesse drank most of his iced tea and gestured to the waitress. She poured him some more. He added some sugar and drank another swallow and looked at Sunny.

"No," he said. "I wasn't."

"Does that bother you?"

"That I wasn't enough?" Jesse said.

Sunny nodded.

"A lot," Jesse said.

"Think it's why you drink?" Sunny said.

Jesse was silent for a moment, looking at his iced tea.

"I think I always drank too much," Jesse said. "But it got away from me when Jenn and I started having problems."

"How you doing now?"

"Pretty good," Jesse said. "Normally I have a couple at night after work, before I have supper. I haven't been drunk for a long time."

Sunny reached across and patted his hand.

"Why do you—" she said.

Jesse's cell phone rang.

"Excuse me," he said, and answered it.

He listened for a moment.

"Okay," he said. "I'll come along."

He looked at Sunny.

"Business?" she said.

"Yes."

"Go ahead," Sunny said. "I'll take care of the check."

"That doesn't seem right," Jesse said.

"Spike has never charged me for a meal," Sunny said. "I sign the check, and he tears it up."

Jesse stood.

"Boston, too?"

"Boston," Sunny said, "here, doesn't matter. Spike loves me."

"Maybe I should try that," he said.

"Spike doesn't love you," Sunny said.

"But he does you?" Jesse said.

"Totally," Sunny said.

"Spike's gay," Jesse said.

"True," Sunny said. "So he doesn't want to have sex, but he loves me."

"Some men might do both," Jesse said.

"Anyone in mind?"

"We'll talk," Jesse said. "You had a question before the phone rang?"

"It can wait," Sunny said. "Go be chief of police."

"I'm always the chief of police," Jesse said.

"Even in a dressing room in a boutique on Rodeo Drive?"

Jesse smiled.

"Except then," he said.

5

SUNNY DECIDED TO VISIT the Renewal on her own. She had
an address, and she knew it was in the neighborhood. She
walked up the low-rise of Front Street from the wharf, along
the harbor front. Jesse was so much like her ex-husband. Both
of them contained, and interior, and physically competent.
Both of them, maybe, a little dangerous. Her father was like
that, too. She smiled.

What a coincidence, I'm attracted to men like my father.

But all that competence and grace, she thought, was exter-
ior, and inside—confusion. At least in Jesse's case. At least
about love.

Most of the houses along this stretch of waterfront in the
oldest part of town looked as if they'd been rehabbed recently

by people with money. They didn't seem very interesting from the street side. They all appeared oriented toward the harbor.

An ocean view, Sunny thought, *like our first house. . . . It wasn't that far from here. . . . I wonder what Richie is like inside.*

She stopped walking.

I don't know, she thought. *I have no idea. . . . I have no idea what Richie was, or is, like inside. . . . Daddy, either . . . Except I know Daddy loves me. . . . I think maybe Richie does, too . . . or did. . . . I know more about Jesse than I know about anyone. . . . That has to mean something.*

A white-haired woman passed, walking an energetic beagle.

"Are you all right, miss?" the lady said.

Sunny nodded.

"Yes, ma'am," Sunny said. "Thank you. I was just thinking."

"Oh, my," the lady said. "We mustn't do too much of that."

Sunny smiled at her.

"No," Sunny said, "we probably shouldn't."

The beagle scrabbled on the sidewalk at the end of the leash.

"Oh, all right, Sally," the woman said to the dog, and let the beagle pull her off toward town.

Sunny looked after them. She'd had to put her dog down a year and a half ago.

I miss my Rose, she thought.

She began to walk again, but slowly, as if she had no destination.

But I know a lot about what Jesse is like inside, more than I know about my father or the man I married . . . except I don't know if he loves me . . . or can.

17

The smell of the harbor was strong. She couldn't see much of it because the houses were very close along here; waterfront property was very expensive, no reason to waste any. She shook her head and laughed to herself without humor.

Of course, I don't know if I love him . . . or can.

Ahead of her was the uninteresting back of a gray shingled house that was right up against the sidewalk. There were a few small windows and a blank red door that faced the street. On the door was the number 17 in brass. The address of the Bond of the Renewal. When she reached the door, Sunny stopped and looked at it. There was a tiny passageway on each side of the house, which separated it from the adjacent houses. Sunny estimated she could turn sideways and get through, but she was pretty sure Spike couldn't.

Do I want to go in there now. . . . No, I don't. . . . Do I want to swap small talk with the Renewal. . . . Not today . . . Right now I want to walk along the street some more and think of how fucked-up Jesse's life is . . . and mine . . . and pretty much everything god- damned else.

She turned and walked back toward the Gray Gull at the foot of the long gradual downhill return.

I think all I ever understood was Rosie.

6

PETER PERKINS CAME INTO Jesse's office, carrying a cup of coffee in one hand and a manila folder in the other. He put the coffee on the edge of Jesse's desk, sat down in one of the visitors' chairs, and opened the folder.

"ME's report?" Jesse said.

"Yep, on Petrov Ognowski."

"So it was his car," Jesse said.

"Yep. ID'ed him with his fingerprints. Got a big record. Shot once in the back of the head with a .22 slug, probably a Magnum load, the way it churned around inside his skull."

"Identifiable?" Jesse said.

"Nope, too beat up. ME says they could barely tell it was a .22, the way it was twisted out of shape."

"Happens," Jesse said. "Got a time of death?"

"Tuesday night between midnight and six."

"Anything else?"

"Not much. Petrov might have gone happy, though. He had sex earlier Tuesday evening."

"You ever wonder how they know that?" Jesse said.

Perkins looked startled.

"You don't know?"

"Not a clue," Jesse said.

Perkins looked even more startled.

He said, "Some kind of science, I guess."

"Probably is," Jesse said. "What else do we know about Mr. Ognowski?"

"He's a soldier with a mob headed by a guy named Reggie Galen. Strong-arm mostly. Arrested six times for assault. Served some time for extortion."

"Where'd he do time," Jesse said.

"Garrison."

"See what they can tell you about him," Jesse said.

Perkins made a note in his folder.

"You know where Reggie lives?" Jesse said.

"Here."

"On the Neck," Jesse said.

"In the old Stackpole house," Perkins said, "next door to Knocko Moynihan."

"Who bought the old Winthrop house," Jesse said.

"There goes the neighborhood," Perkins said.

"Unless you're a thug," Jesse said.

"Why do you suppose they did that?" Perkins said. "Moved in next door to one another."

"My dick is bigger than yours, I suppose," Jesse said.

"They don't get along, do they?"

"I don't believe so," Jesse said.

"Well," Perkins said. "Gives us a nice passel of suspects to talk with."

"None of whom will be able to shed any light on the unfortunate crime."

"Yeah," Perkins said. "Trouble with gang murders is nobody sees anything, knows anything. All of them got lawyers."

Jesse smiled. Perkins was a good kid, but Jesse wondered just how many gang murders he'd worked on. Perkins saw the smile.

"Don't you think?" he said.

"I do," Jesse said. "He have a gun on him?"

"Ognowski? No."

"In the car?" Jesse said.

"No."

"Any kind of weapon?" Jesse said.

"No," Perkins said. "That mean something?"

"Guys in his profession," Jesse said, "usually like to be carrying something."

"So, what's it mean that he wasn't?"

"Don't know," Jesse said. "It's a little odd, so we mark it, you know?"

"Yessir," Perkins said. "You gonna talk with Reggie Galen?"

"I'll talk to Healy first, see what the staties know."

"And I'll get hold of somebody at Garrison," Perkins said.

"Good," Jesse said.

"We got a theory of the case yet?" Perkins said.

"Somebody shot Petrov and put him in his trunk," Jesse said.

"Wow," Perkins said. "It's great to work with a professional."

"I know," Jesse said. "I know."

7

NEED A DRINK," Sunny said, as she came through Jesse's
front door.

"Martini?"

"Yes."

Jesse made her a martini and himself a scotch and soda and
brought the drinks into the living room. Sunny drank nearly
half of hers. Jesse raised his eyebrows.

"Hey," he said. "I'm the boozer around here."

"Richie's wife had a son. Richard Felix Burke, seven pounds,
four ounces."

Jesse nodded.

"Drink up," he said.

Sunny sat for a time in silence. Jesse was silent with her.

Then she said, "Richie called me. He sounded so excited. So happy."

"Must be an exciting thing," Jesse said.

"It's over," Sunny said.

"You and Richie?"

"Yes," she said. "I know him. He will never leave his son or his son's mother."

Jesse nodded. Sunny drank the rest of her martini. Jesse stood to make her another one.

"No," Sunny said. "I don't want to get drunk. I just needed some kind of little jolt to help me get past this."

"The jolt work?" Jesse said.

"No."

"Generally doesn't," he said.

"Several more jolts won't work, either," Sunny said.

"Probably not," Jesse said.

"At least the roller coaster is over," Sunny said. "We're apart, we might get together, we might not, we might. At least we have closure. Excuse the dreadful cliché."

"Excused," Jesse said. "You want to stay here tonight?"

Sunny shook her head.

"I couldn't."

"No ulterior motives," Jesse said. "I can sleep on the couch."

"Thank you, but no," Sunny said. "I think I need to be alone. . . . May as well get used to it."

"You may not be with Richie," Jesse said. "But you won't be alone."

Sunny smiled.

"Thank you."

They were quiet. Then Sunny stood and walked over to Jesse and kissed him gently on the mouth and straightened and walked out through the front door and closed it gently behind her. Jesse heard her heels go down the outside stairs, and she was gone.

He still had most of his drink left. He sipped it slowly, looking at the big photo of Ozzie Smith stretched parallel to the infield, catching a line drive. Then he got up and made another drink and walked with it to the French doors that opened onto the little balcony that overlooked the harbor. He didn't go out. He sipped his drink and looked at the dark water.

Then he raised the half-drunk glass of scotch.

"Good luck, Richard Felix Burke," he said, and drank.

I T WAS SEVEN O'CLOCK in the evening when Healy came into Jesse's office.

"You ever go home," Healy said.

"Sometimes," Jesse said. "To sleep. How 'bout you?"

"On my way," Healy said.

He sat down and put his briefcase on the floor beside him.

"You wanted to know about the late Petrov Ognowski and his employer?" Healy said.

"Reggie Galen," Jesse said.

"Course you know Reggie lives here," Healy said.

"Right next door to Knocko Moynihan," Jesse said.

Healy nodded.

"How weird is that," he said.

"They do any business together?"

"None that I know of, now," Healy said. "I talked with some guys in our OC unit. None that they know of."

"But they're not enemies," Jesse said.

"Not that I know of," Healy said. "Or OC knows."

"And you'd know," Jesse said.

"I am a captain in the Massachusetts State Police," Healy said.

"So there's nothing you wouldn't know," Jesse said.

"This is correct."

"Could you focus this vast knowledge in," Jesse said. "Ognowski, say, and his boss?"

"Ognowski's a thumper, or he was," Healy said.

He bent over, opened his briefcase, took out an eight-by-ten photograph, and put it on Jesse's desk.

"You want somebody killed, or maimed, or scared, whatever," Healy said, "Petrov is your guy. He was working for Reggie Galen before his tragic demise."

Jesse looked at the picture.

"Good-looking guy," Jesse said. "Face doesn't look like he lost many fights."

"Petrov could always find employment," Healy said.

"Was he with Reggie for long?"

"You know how it goes with these guys," Healy said. "They work for a while, they go away. They come back. We don't have the resources to keep track of everybody, and low-life boppers don't get all that much of our time. Best I can tell you, he's been with Reggie the last several years."

"He ever work for Knocko?"

"Don't know," Healy said. "You don't like them being neighbors, do you?"

"Coincidences don't work for me," Jesse said.

"Me, either."

"But you got no explanation," Jesse said.

"No."

"And you a captain," Jesse said. "What about Reggie?"

"Reggie had a good piece of the action in the North End and Charlestown, Everett, Revere, Malden. We tag-teamed him with the Feds, turned some witnesses, and sent him away for five."

"You like working with the Feds?" Jesse said.

Healy shrugged.

"Lot of 'em ain't really street cops," Healy said. "But they got great information."

"They got the money to pay for it," Jesse said.

"And they do," Healy said.

He took a manila envelope out of his briefcase and put it next to Ognowski's picture on Jesse's desk.

"Names and numbers are in there," Healy said. "Read 'em at your leisure."

Jesse nodded.

"When did he get out of jail?"

"Twelve years ago," Healy said.

"Back in business?" Jesse said.

"Sort of," Healy said. "We can't prove it yet. But as far as we can tell, he's like some sort of warlord, you know. He gets a skim off every bet made, every whore bought, every joint smoked, every number purchased, every loan sharked. He gets this everywhere he used to run things. So he doesn't have to do much, just be Reggie Galen, and the cash just keeps on coming."

"And if it doesn't?"

"He has members of his staff," Healy said, "go and collect it."

"Which was where Ognowski comes in."

"Yep. Got a bunch of Ognowskis," Healy said. "They protect and collect, you might say."

"And Knocko's got no part of it?"

"Don't know," Healy said. "When you called you didn't ask me about Knocko. He hasn't shown up in the morning report anytime recent."

"Well, maybe I'll find out something," Jesse said.

"You gonna talk to them?"

"I'll go visit Reggie, see what develops."

"Something you need to keep in mind," Healy said. "I know it, and a couple of the OC boys mentioned it. Reggie's a slick item. He's quite pleasant, seems like a good guy, easygoing. But he ain't. I don't know if he'd kill a cop, but I don't know that he wouldn't. Depends on how bad he needs to, I think. I don't know if he's got a soul or not. But I know he's got no conscience."

"How about fear?" Jesse said. "He got any of that?"

"He can cause it, but no, I don't think he's afraid of much."

Jesse grinned.

"Wait'll he gets a load of me," he said.

Healy nodded slowly.

"That's what worries me," he said.

9

THE TWO GATED ESTATES stood side by side on the open
Atlantic side of Paradise Neck. They looked as if someone
had flipped a picture. Both were rambling gray-shingled man-
sions whose focus was the ocean that broke against the foot of
their sloping backyards. Each had a long driveway that curved
up around the house to a parking area at the top. The driveways
and parking areas were both cobblestone. Jesse couldn't remember who had moved there first. Who was copying whom? The
flower beds were similar. The shade trees were similar. There
were blue hydrangeas growing near each front porch.

The gate to Reggie Galen's house was closed. Jesse stopped
with the nose of his car at the gate. Inside the gate, on the left,
there was a guard shack disguised as a small carriage house.

One of its two doors opened on Jesse's side of the gate, and a tall man with a good tan and salt-and-pepper hair came out. He was wearing aviator sunglasses and a white shirt with epaulets, with the shirttails out, over dark slacks.

"May I help you?" he said.

"My name is Jesse Stone," Jesse said. "I'm the chief of police here in Paradise, and I am here to see Mr. Galen."

"What is your business with Mr. Galen," the guard said.

"Police," Jesse said.

The guard nodded thoughtfully.

"I don't think Mr. Galen's much interested in police business," the guard said.

"You got a license for that piece?" Jesse said.

"A license?" the guard said.

"A license to carry."

"I ain't carrying," the guard said.

"Yeah," Jesse said, "you are, right hip, under the shirttail."

The guard looked at Jesse. Jesse looked at the guard.

"May I see your gun license?" Jesse said.

"Lemme call up to the house," the guard said. "Tell 'em you're coming."

"Sure," Jesse said.

By the time he had driven up over the cobblestones and parked in the turnaround beside the house, two guys in seersucker sport coats and pink Lacoste polo shirts were standing on the side porch. Jesse got out and walked toward them.

"Chief Stone," one of them said.

He was a pleasant-looking man, about Jesse's size. He was clean shaven and tanned and had a nice, healthy look about him.

"Here to see Mr. Galen," Jesse said.

"Chief of all the police?" the other man said. "In this whole big town?"

This man was younger and bigger, a bodybuilder with a crew cut and a tiny beard that occupied about two triangular inches below his bottom lip. Jesse looked at him for a moment without saying anything.

"You have a gun," the older man said.

"I do," Jesse said.

"Generally we're not supposed to let anyone bring a gun inside," the older man said.

"But there's probably an exception for chiefs of police," Jesse said.

"I don't see no reason for exceptions," the younger man said.

The older man looked at him and then at Jesse and rolled his eyes.

"Normie," he said. "It ain't always wise to start up with the cops."

Normie snorted.

"What kind of cop work you do?" Normie said. "Bust people for clamming out of season?"

"What's your name?" Jesse said to the older man.

"Bob Davis," the man said.

"Can we stop horsing around with Joe Palooka here and go on in and see Mr. Galen?"

"What's that mean?" Normie said. "What's he mean, Joe Palooka?"

Bob smiled and shook his head.

"The perfect combo," he said to Jesse. "Stupid and aggressive."

"Hey," Normie said. "Who you—"

Bob looked at him and said, *"Shhh."*

Normie stopped.

"Stay here," Bob said to Normie.

Then he looked at Jesse and nodded for him to head toward the porch door. *Bob's got a little clout,* Jesse thought, as he followed him through the door.

REGGIE GALEN and his wife were having coffee together on their back deck, under a white awning, watching the iron-colored waves break against the rust-colored rocks at the foot of their lawn.

"Chief Stone," Bob said. "Mr. and Mrs. Galen."

Galen glanced up at Jesse and nodded. Mrs. Galen stood and put out her hand.

"Hi," she said. "I'm Rebecca Galen."

"Jesse Stone."

"Would you like some coffee?"

"I would," Jesse said.

She poured him some from a silver pot.

"Cream? Sugar?"

"Both," Jesse said. "Three sugars."

She gestured toward a chair.

"Please," she said.

When he was seated across from Reggie, she handed him his coffee. Rebecca poured more coffee into her husband's cup and a little more into her own. Then she sat down next to her husband and patted his forearm. Bob stood back a little and watched.

"You can go, Bobby," Reggie said.

Bob nodded and left without a word.

"I love Bob," Rebecca said.

Her husband grinned at her.

"Maybe I better get rid of him," he said.

"No need," Rebecca said. "I love you more."

"Whaddya thinka that," Reggie said to Jesse. "Woman like her saying things like that to me."

"Glad to see you're happy," Jesse said.

"Oh," Rebecca said, "we are."

Reggie nodded. Rebecca was a knockout in white shorts and a black top. Dark hair cut shorter in the back than the front. Tan skin, big eyes, wide mouth. She was slim, but she looked strong. Reggie was tall and big-boned. He had a square face and an aggressive nose.

"So," Reggie said. "How'd you know my guy at the gate had a gun on his right hip?"

"I guessed," Jesse said.

"And you guessed he was right-handed?"

"Most people are, and he was wearing a watch on his left wrist."

"Wow," Reggie said. "No wonder you made chief."

"It was nothing," Jesse said.

"What would you have done if you were wrong?"

"I'da thought of something else," Jesse said.

"I'll bet you would. Whaddya need?"

"Petrov Ognowski," Jesse said.

"What about him?"

"He's dead," Jesse said.

"Petey?"

"Somebody shot him in the back of the head. Probably with a .22 Mag," Jesse said.

"When?" Reggie said.

Jesse told him. Rebecca stopped rubbing Reggie's forearm but left her hand resting on top of his.

"Goddamn," Reggie said. "I wondered where he was."

"Ognowski worked for you."

"Yes."

"Doing what?"

"Security," Reggie said.

"Like Bob," Jesse said.

"Sort of," Reggie said. "Bob's, like, my guy. Petey was more like Normie and the guy at the gate. They took direction from Bob."

"And Bob takes direction from you?"

"Me and Becca," Reggie said.

"You got any idea why Petey got shot?" Jesse said.

"No," Reggie said. "Let's not bullshit each other. You know, and I know, I was in the rackets. You know, and I know, I done time. And you know, and I know, that everybody thinks I'm still in the rackets."

"Which he isn't," Rebecca said.

"And if he were?" Jesse said.

"I married him when he was," Rebecca said.

"And if he were again?" Jesse said.

"I married him forever," Rebecca said.

"How long you been married?" Jesse said.

He had no idea where he was going. But he had plenty of time.

"Twenty-one years," Rebecca said.

"Wow," Jesse said. "You're older than you look."

"I was twenty," she said.

"Kids?"

"No."

Jesse nodded and drank coffee.

Then he said, "How'd you folks end up next door to Knocko Moynihan? Everybody thinks he's in the rackets, too."

"I know," Reggie said. "He's married to Becca's sister."

"And you're close with your sister," Jesse said.

"Identical twins," Rebecca said.

"Close," Jesse said.

Both Rebecca and Reggie nodded.

"Think Knocko knows anything about what happened to Petey?" Jesse said.

"Might ask him," Reggie said. "Knocko knows a lot."

"And you don't," Jesse said.

Reggie smiled.

"I know a lot, too," he said. "Just not about this."

THE PATRIARCH of the Bond of the Renewal dyed his hair. It was the first thing Sunny knew for sure as she sat in the kitchen of the Renewal House and drank some tea with him. Without sugar.

"We don't allow sugar in the Renewal," the Patriarch said. "It's a stimulant."

"And the tea is not?" Sunny said.

"The tea is soothing," the Patriarch said. "It quiets the soul."

"I didn't know that," Sunny said.

The Patriarch smiled.

He was wearing a white linen shirt and white linen pants with reverse pleats. There were tan leather sandals on his feet. He appeared to have had a recent pedicure.

"You will probably find several of our practices amusing. But they all conspire to make us what we are."

"I'm hoping to chat with Cheryl DeMarco," Sunny said.

The Patriarch nodded. He was a smallish man with a smooth, pleasant face and some shoulder-length silver hair that must have taken some frequent color work to maintain.

"Why?" he said.

"Her parents want her to come home."

"You are a private detective?" the Patriarch said.

"Yes."

"May I see something that says so?"

"Sure," Sunny said, and gave him something.

He read and nodded.

"You are not, I hope"—he wrinkled his nose and pursed his lips as if he'd encountered a bad smell—"a deprogrammer."

"No," Sunny said. "Probably don't believe in it, and if I did I wouldn't know how to go about it."

"That's a relief," the Patriarch said. "I can understand why her parents would want her home. Most parents want their children home. But why not simply ask her. Why hire you?"

"They think you are a bunch of whackdoodles," Sunny said.

"Whackdoodles," the Patriarch said.

"Whackdoodles," Sunny said.

The Patriarch smiled.

"I must say, you are direct."

"Surely you must be used to it. A lot of people must think you're odd."

He nodded.

"They do," he said. "And I find it puzzling. There's nothing particularly odd in our teachings."

"What are your teachings," Sunny said.

"We believe in a pervasive benign spiritual presence in the universe. We feel no need to define it more exactly. We believe it is manifest in every aspect of daily life, if one will but pay attention. We oppose anything that clouds our perception of that spirit. We oppose anything that clouds our ability to connect to this spirit. We don't drink alcohol or coffee. We don't permit drug use, including nicotine. We don't believe living creatures should suffer for us, so we are vegetarians."

"No sympathy for the poor turnip?" Sunny said.

"You're teasing, I know. But we are aware that without death, there can be no life. It is a central myth of most religions."

"Death and rebirth," Sunny said.

"Of course," the Patriarch said. "Are you an educated person?"

"I don't know," Sunny said. "I went to college."

"So, yes," the Patriarch said. "We have to consume other living things, or we die. But we try to keep the consumption at the lower end of the chain of being."

He shrugged.

"It's the best we can do," he said.

"You haven't mentioned your teachings on sex," Sunny said. "It's a hot subject with parents."

"Ah, yes," the Patriarch said. "Sex."

"That one," Sunny said.

"Let me ask you what you believe."

"About sex?"

"Yes."

Sunny smiled.

"I like it," she said.

"Yes, most of us do as well. We believe in consenting adults. We believe in sex as an expression of affection, and we disapprove of sex as an expression of pathology."

"Well," Sunny said. "I can certainly see why her parents are horrified."

The Patriarch looked genuinely startled.

"You can?"

"Sarcasm," Sunny said.

"Oh, excuse me," the Patriarch said. "I am often too earnest."

"Better than the reverse," Sunny said. "Where do you get your funding?"

"I am quite wealthy," the Patriarch said.

"Is this your house?"

"It is."

"How'd you get wealthy," Sunny said.

"I inherited my parents' wealth," he said.

"No heavy lifting," Sunny said.

"My parents were a pretty heavy burden when they were alive," the Patriarch said. "But no, I've never had to scramble for money."

"Parents can be a heavy burden even when they are no longer alive," Sunny said.

"So the psychiatrists would have you believe," the Patriarch said.

"But you don't believe them?"

"Psychiatry is superfluous," the Patriarch said. "If we open our soul and simplify our life, the benevolence of the universe will flow into us."

Sunny nodded.

"Would it be possible to speak with Cheryl DeMarco?"

"Of course," the Patriarch said.

12

SUNNY SAT WITH CHERYL and her boyfriend on the patio in the front of the house, where below them in the harbor sailboats bobbed at their moorings and fishing boats went purposefully. The boyfriend was a tall, husky blond kid with a blank, sincere face. He sat beside Cheryl and held her hand.

"This here is Todd," Cheryl said. "He's my boyfriend."

"Nice to meet you, Todd," Sunny said.

Todd nodded a hard-bitten nod. He was there, Sunny realized, to prevent her from throwing Cheryl over her shoulder and dashing off.

"Are you, honest to God, a private eye?" Cheryl said.

She was small and soft, with a smooth, round face, no makeup, and straight blond hair that hung to her shoulders.

"Honest to God," Sunny said.

"You got a gun?"

"I do," Sunny said.

"Where?"

"In my purse," Sunny said. "Sometimes I tuck it into my stocking top if I'm expecting action."

"You're not wearing stockings," Cheryl said.

"A weak attempt at humor," Sunny said. "Purse is fine."

"How'd you get to be a private eye," Cheryl said.

The boyfriend watched Sunny closely.

"My father is a retired police captain," Sunny said. "I was a police officer for a while. . . . Just seemed a good idea at the time."

"You married?"

"No."

"Ever been?"

"Yes."

"What happened?"

"None of your business," Sunny said.

The boyfriend looked at her harder. Cheryl shrugged.

"Just asking," she said.

Sunny nodded.

"You like it here?" Sunny said.

"I can't believe they hired a detective to come talk to me," Cheryl said.

Sunny nodded.

"So," she said. "How do you like it here?"

"Here?"

Sunny nodded brightly.

"Here," she said.

"It's very cool here, isn't it, Todd?"

The boyfriend nodded.

"What's the coolest part of it," Sunny said.

"No hassle," Cheryl said. "Everyone here is really, you know, mellowed out."

"No rules," Sunny said.

"Well, a'course, there gotta be rules," Cheryl said.

"What are they?"

"No drugs, no alcohol, no smoking," Cheryl said. "No meanness."

" 'No meanness'?" Sunny said.

"You know, no being mean to anybody."

"Oh," Sunny said. "And if you break the rules?"

"The group has a gathering," Cheryl said, "and decides."

"What's the worst punishment?"

"You have to leave the group."

"How about sex," Sunny said. "Any rules on that?"

"You think sex is bad?"

"No," Sunny said. "I like it."

Cheryl looked faintly startled.

"They got no rules on sex," she said. "As long as you keep it real."

" 'Real'?"

"You know, with somebody you, like, love," Cheryl said.

Sunny nodded. Nothing conflicted with the Patriarch's version.

"So, you're here because you want to be," Sunny said.

"Exactly," Cheryl said. "I'm with Todd. We got friends, a life, stuff to do, people to help us."

"How 'bout twenty years from now?" Sunny said.

Cheryl stared at her for a moment.

"When you were eighteen," Cheryl said, "were you worrying about twenty years later?"

Sunny smiled.

"No," she said. "I wasn't."

"So?" Cheryl said.

"Good point," Sunny said.

She stood.

"Todd," she said, "I want to whisper a couple things to Cheryl over by the railing there. Girl stuff, might be a little embarrassing."

Todd shrugged as if he knew just what she meant. Sunny beckoned Cheryl and walked to the railing. Below in the harbor, someone's yacht, sails loosely furled, was edging in toward the town landing under power. Cheryl came and stood beside her.

"Anything you want to say that Todd can't hear?" Sunny said softly.

"Todd? He's my boyfriend."

"I understand," Sunny said. "But I just need to be sure. Is there any restraint on your leaving?"

"I don't want to leave."

Sunny nodded. "I know that, too," she said. "But if you did want to leave, would there be anything to prevent you?"

"No," Cheryl said.

"And you don't want to leave?"

"God, no."

"I'll take you out now if you want to go," Sunny said.

"I don't want to go," Cheryl said. "Why won't you believe me?"

"I do believe you," Sunny said. "I just have to be sure."

"Well, be sure," Cheryl said, and turned away and walked back to sit beside Todd.

Sunny followed and stood in front of Cheryl.

"If I brought your parents here," Sunny said, "would you talk to them?"

Cheryl made a dismissive sound.

"They aren't going to come here," she said.

"Maybe not," Sunny said. "But if they did?"

"Sure," Cheryl said. "If you stayed with us."

"I will," Sunny said. "But why?"

"They're clueless," Cheryl said.

"And I'm not?"

"You don't seem it," Cheryl said.

"Thank you."

"You're welcome," Cheryl said. "Most grown-ups are clueless."

"Maybe they just know different clues," Sunny said.

"Whatever," Cheryl said. "Doesn't much matter anyway. They are so totally not going to come."

"Let me ask them," Sunny said, "and I'll let you know."

"I don't mind talking to you," Cheryl said.

13

Mrs. Moynihan let Jesse in. She looked just like Rebecca Galen.

"Hi," she said. "I'm Robbie Moynihan."

"Jesse Stone."

"Please come in," Robbie said. "My husband and I were just having coffee. Would you care for some?"

"That would be nice," Jesse said.

"Follow me," she said.

Jesse followed her through the house, which looked very much like the Galens' house. Her backside looked very much like Rebecca's.

"So, whaddya need from me, Stone," Knocko said, when Jesse was seated.

He was a big man gone soft. You could still see what he was, Jesse thought, though it was disappearing fast. Robbie sat beside him and looked attentive as he spoke.

"Fella named Ognowski was killed around here, couple days ago," Jesse said. "We're just canvassing the neighborhood."

Knocko laughed.

"You're canvassing me and Reggie," he said.

"It's where we've begun," Jesse said. "You know Ognowski?"

"Petey? Sure I know him. He worked for my brother-in-law."

"Any reason you know that somebody would kill him?" Jesse said.

"Not a clue," Knocko said. He looked at his wife. "You, sweetheart?"

"Petey." Robbie shook her head. "Petey was the nicest man."

"As leg breakers go," Jesse said.

"That's not so," Robbie said. "Petey was a sweet man."

She smiled at her husband.

"Like Francis," she said.

"Francis," Jesse said.

"My real name," Knocko said.

"Where'd Knocko come from?" Jesse said.

"When I was a kid," Knocko said, "I used to be kind of a rough guy."

"Petey do any work for you?" Jesse said.

"I'm retired," Knocko said. "He used to run some errands now and then for Robbie."

"Like what?" Jesse said.

Knocko looked at his wife.

"Honey?" he said.

"Oh, pick up something at the market, take something to the cleaner's. He did the same for Becca."

"That was it?" Jesse said.

"You know Reggie was in the rackets once," Knocko said. "Everybody knows that. You're in the rackets, even if you ain't anymore, you need some security."

"Which Bob's in charge of," Jesse said. "For Reggie."

"Yeah."

"We all know you were in the rackets once," Jesse said. "Who does your security?"

"*Security*'s kind of a fancy word," Knocko said, and winked at Robbie. "Got a buddy walks around with me."

"What's his name?" Jesse said.

"Ray Mulligan," Knocko said. "Met in grade school. Nuns seated us alphabetically, you know? I was always right next to Ray."

He patted Robbie's arm. She smiled at him.

"You're Rebecca Galen's twin sister," Jesse said.

"Yes, identical twins. Unless we dress differently, even we have trouble telling us apart."

"What was your, ah, birth name?" Jesse said.

"Why you wanna know that?" Knocko said.

"'Cause I don't know," Jesse said. "You been questioned before, Knocko. You know that cops ask questions to see where they lead."

"You ever been a cop anyplace but here?" Knocko said.

"Why you wanna know that?" Jesse said.

"'Cause I don't know," Knocko said.

Jesse smiled.

"I worked robbery homicide in L.A. for a while," Jesse said.

"So you done something but hand out traffic tickets," Knocko said.

"Not much," Jesse said. "What was your maiden name, Mrs. Moynihan?"

She looked at her husband. Knocko nodded.

"Bangston," she said. "Roberta and Rebecca, the Bangston twins."

"And how'd you two meet?" Jesse said.

Knocko shook his head.

He said, "Enough, Stone. You got no reason to suspect us of anything. We got no reason to sit here and blab about our private lives with you."

"I know," Jesse said. "Just curious how twin sisters ended up marrying a couple of thugs like you and Reggie."

"*Thugs* is kind of a harsh word," Knocko said.

"Extralegal entrepreneurs," Jesse said.

"Better," Knocko said.

"You guys ever adversaries?" Jesse said.

"No, no problem with Reggie and me. He had the North Shore. I had the South . . . 'fore we retired."

Jesse shrugged.

"Still kind of odd," he said.

"Are you married, Chief Stone?" Robbie said.

"No."

"Ever been?" she said.

"Yes," he said.

"Then perhaps you have noticed," Robbie said, "that love is odd."

"I have," Jesse said.

14

JESSE MADE his first drink of the day carefully. Tall glass, a lot of ice, not too much scotch, a lot of soda. If he got it right, it always resulted in a nice drink that made him feel fresh.

He took the glass to his living room and sat at the bar. He raised his glass toward the picture of Ozzie Smith.

"Howya doing, Wizard," he said, and took a swallow.

He'd done it right; it was dry and clean and cold.

The room was silent except for the soft sound of the air-conditioning, which somehow made everything seem more silent. He drank again, looking across his living room and through the French doors at the diminishing daylight that now had a faint blue tinge to it. He liked the silence, and the bluish light, and being alone. He might have liked being alone more if there was someone else in the house, or expected home.

"Maybe I should get a dog," Jesse said.

He drank.

"Except who takes care of it when I'm working. If I had a wife, she could take care of it. But if I had a wife, I wouldn't need the dog."

He drank.

"I'd want a dog anyway," Jesse said.

Ozzie Smith had no reaction. Jesse's glass was empty. He went to the kitchen and made another. He felt like getting drunk. Why was that? Often he was happy with a couple of drinks and supper. He took his drink back to the living room.

"Who's here to tell me no?" Jesse said.

What would Dix say? Jesse would say that if behavior changed, there was probably a reason for it. And he would say he had no way to know what that reason was. But Jesse knew Dix would think it was still about Jenn.

"The hell with Jenn," Jesse said.

So why today, and not, say, two days ago, or last Thursday. Why tonight did he feel pretty sure he wouldn't settle for two drinks?

He looked at Ozzie Smith again.

"I'da made the show, Oz," Jesse said. "Hadn't busted up my shoulder, I'd have made the show."

He took a swallow.

"I'm a good cop, too . . . sober."

How did it happen that two thugs like Galen and Moynihan

ended up with two beautiful women who seemed devoted to them? And he had ended up with Jenn.

"Whoops," he said.

He put his drink down and sat back in is chair. . . . That's why he wanted to get drunk.

He was jealous. . . . No, jealous wasn't quite it. . . . He had seen the marriage he wished he'd had, and he'd seen two of them in two days. It underscored the failure of his own marriage. They had gotten women who wanted to make their husbands happy. He'd gotten one who wanted to be famous. He was an honest cop. They were mobsters.

He went to the kitchen and made himself another drink.

Love is odd, all right . . . and unfair . . . and it sucks. . . . Doesn't always suck, though. Working really well for Reggie and Knocko . . . Thought I was through worrying about it . . . Jenn's history . . . Thought I was past that . . . Guess I'm not . . . Maybe I can drink it into submission.

He drank some more.

THE PHONE RANG. Jesse ignored it. His mouth was very dry, but he was too asleep to get any water. The phone rang again.

"Shut up," Jesse said, and didn't answer it.

He slept some more and then someone began pounding on his front door. He ignored it. The pounding continued. He could hear someone's raised voice. He rolled over onto his back and opened his eyes. It was day. He looked at the digital clock: eleven-thirteen.

His head ached and his stomach was queasy. The pounding and yelling at the front door continued. He sat up. He was fully dressed, shoes and all. He stood. The room swam a little and then steadied. He walked slowly to the front door and opened it. Molly Crane was there. She looked at Jesse and then came in without a word and closed the door behind her.

"Take a shower," she said. "Put on clean clothes. I'll make coffee."

Jesse looked at her for a moment.

"Wha's up," he said.

"Brush your teeth, too," Molly said.

Jesse nodded.

"Okay, but wha's going on?" he said.

"Somebody killed Knocko Moynihan last night," Molly said.

Jesse nodded, then turned and headed for the bathroom. He brushed his teeth. He shaved. He stayed under the shower for a long time. When he came out wearing clean clothes, Molly had coffee made, a glass of orange juice poured, two pieces of toast on a saucer. A bottle of aspirin stood beside the toast. Jesse sat.

"No toast," Jesse said.

"Eat the toast," Molly said. "Shape your stomach must be in, you don't want to put aspirin in there without food."

Jesse nodded. The room distorted for a moment and settled. He drank some juice.

"Feel human?" Molly said.

"No," Jesse said.

"Can you listen?"

"Yes," he said.

"Lifeguard found Knocko this morning, about six o'clock, sitting upright on a bench under the little pavilion at Paradise Beach. He'd been shot in the back of the head. There wasn't much blood. We're guessing he was shot someplace else and put there. But we don't have an ME report yet."

Jesse drank some coffee to wash down a bite of toast.

"Who's running it?" he said.

"Suit, I guess, and me," Molly said. "Selectmen are in a twid-git looking for you."

"Press?"

"Quite a bit," Molly said. "Knocko was famous, I guess."

"TV?" Jesse said.

"Two stations," Molly said. "Stand-ups by the beach pavilion."

"Scared to death of TV," Jesse said.

"The selectmen?"

Jesse nodded and wished he hadn't.

"'Specially the new guy," Molly said.

Jesse started to nod and stopped himself.

"McAfee," he said.

"Yeah," Molly said. "He's terrified he'll say something wrong on camera."

Jesse finished his first piece of toast.

"Okay," Molly said. "Take your aspirin."

Jesse took two and swallowed them with the remaining orange juice.

"He know where I've been?" Jesse said.

"Suit told them you were out of town, something to do with your ex-wife."

"Better than passed out from strong drink, I guess," Jesse said.

"I guess," Molly said.

She poured Jesse a second cup of coffee.

"You going to eat the other piece of toast?" she said.

"Can't," Jesse said.

"I can," Molly said, and picked it up from his plate and broke off a piece.

"Someday you can tell me what set you off," Molly said, when she had finished chewing.

"Yep."

"But right now we got to rescue the situation," Molly said.

"Okay," Jesse said.

"You up to it?"

"After this coffee," Jesse said.

Molly nodded and ate the rest of the toast.

16

SUNNY SAT in the vast ornamental living room of a dispropor-
tionate McMansion in Concord with Elsa and John Markham.

"You've talked to our daughter?" Elsa said.

"I have."

"How is she?"

"She seems fine," Sunny said.

"She's still in that place," Elsa said.

Elsa Markham was slim and tall with silver-blond hair and
a dark tan. Her husband was also slim and tall. But his hair was
dark and worn longish. He, too, had a deep tan.

"Yes," Sunny said. "She's at the Renewal place."

"Does she have friends?"

"She has a boyfriend," Sunny said. "He seemed nice."

He hadn't seemed anything to Sunny, but she thought it might reassure them.

"Oh, God," Elsa said. "Unsupervised, of course."

"Well, actually," Sunny said, "there's quite a lot of supervision; at least there are quite a few rules. No drugs, no alcohol, no smoking, interestingly enough, no meat."

"Sex?" Elsa said.

"No casual sex," Sunny said. "Only as part of a relationship."

"Well, isn't that sweet," Elsa said.

"They seem to be close," Sunny said.

"Sex is for marriage," Elsa said. "Not for relationships."

"Really?" Sunny said.

"You don't believe that?" Elsa said.

"No," Sunny said. "I guess I don't."

"Well, we do, and we won't have a daughter who believes otherwise."

"But maybe you do," Sunny said.

"She's been corrupted by this cult."

"It's not really a cult, Mrs. Markham. They don't advocate much that most people wouldn't approve of."

"We are not most people," Elsa said.

Sunny looked at Mr. Markham, who so far had sat in grim silence as his wife talked.

"So, is Cheryl your biological daughter, too, Mr. Markham?"

"Of course," he said. "What kind of a question is that?"

"I don't mean to pry," Sunny said. "Although prying is sort of my profession. But why is her name different than yours?"

"Our name was originally DeMarco," Elsa said. "We changed it as John began to make his way in business."

"Why?"

"DeMarco seemed so North End, you know?"

She wrinkled her nose.

"Johnny DeMarco," she said, and shook her head.

"And Cheryl kept her original name?" Sunny said.

"She took it back when she went off with those people," Elsa said. "Legally, she is Cheryl Markham."

Sunny nodded.

"So, I suggested that perhaps you might visit her," Sunny said. "Talk about this."

"What a dandy idea," Elsa said, and lapsed into a mimicky voice. "'Would you and John care to join us on the Vineyard this weekend?' 'No, we're going to visit our daughter at her free-love hippie commune.' 'Oh, really? How nice. Our daughters are at Wellesley.'"

"Okay," Sunny said. "Not an idea that resonates."

"No," Elsa said. "It's not. Have you any others?"

Her husband had folded his arms and dropped his chin and looked even grimmer. *He's learned every pose,* Sunny thought.

"No," Sunny said. "Do you?"

"John?" Elsa said.

"I got an idea," John said. "You send me a bill for your time, and then go about your business."

"I don't wish to have an argument, but I would point out that you didn't hire me."

"Mistakes are inevitable," John said. "But smart people don't nurture them. Send me a bill and then leave us alone."

"And your daughter?" Sunny said.

"We will tend to our daughter."

He stood. Elsa stood. Sunny nodded and stood. No one offered to shake hands.

As she drove her car down the long driveway, she spoke to herself out loud.

"Wow!" she said.

IT WAS LATE AFTERNOON when Jesse went to Dix's office, but Dix looked as if he'd just stepped out of the shower. His bald head gleamed. His face seemed newly shaved. His seersucker jacket appeared freshly ironed. His white shirt was crisp. He wore a blue-and-yellow striped tie, perfectly knotted.

He nodded as Jesse sat down, and leaned back slightly in his chair as if settling in to listen with interest.

"I got drunk two nights ago and passed out and wasn't able to do my job the next day," Jesse said.

"That must be painful for you," Dix said.

"It is."

"Tell me about it," Dix said.

Jesse told him. Dix listened quietly.

"What do you suppose brought it on?" Dix said.

"All I can think of," Jesse said. "I was talking to a couple of mobsters who seem to be enjoying very happy marriages to some very appealing women."

"Hardly seems fair," Dix said.

Jesse nodded.

"And I guess I sat there, the other night," he said, "and thought, *Why them, not me?* And got drunk."

"Why couldn't Jenn have been like these women?" Dix said.

Jesse nodded.

"Exactly," he said.

Dix was quiet. Jesse was quiet.

"What are they like?" Dix said, after a time.

"The wives?"

Dix nodded.

"They're twins," Jesse said. "Identical twins."

Dix waited.

"They live side by side in big houses on Paradise Neck. Houses look alike, inside and outside. Like they were decorated, or whatever, by the same person."

"Pretty close," Dix said.

Jesse nodded.

Dix waited.

"They're very good-looking," Jesse said.

Dix nodded.

"And they love their husbands."

Dix waited. Jesse was quiet.

"How do you know?" Dix said.

"They are so attentive," Jesse said. "They sit beside their husband. They pat his arm. They look at him and listen to him and seem thrilled to be with him."

"Attentive," Dix said.

"Yes."

"Affectionate," Dix said.

"Yes."

"How about the husbands?" Dix said.

"Reggie Galen," Jesse said. "And Knocko Moynihan. Both mobsters. Reggie ran things mostly north, and Knocko had the South Shore."

"They still in the business?" Dix said.

"They say not, but I don't believe them."

"Why were you talking to them?"

"Guy worked for one of them, slugger named Petrov Ognowski, got killed and his body dumped on the Paradise Neck causeway."

"And you talked to the other man why?"

"He lived next door," Jesse said. "He had a record."

"Any reason to think they were involved?"

"No reason to think anything yet," Jesse said. "You used to be a cop. Guy gets killed in the neighborhood of two mobsters, you talk to them."

Dix nodded.

"These gentlemen seem to recognize their good fortune?" Dix said.

"In their wives, you mean?"

Dix nodded.

"They seem happy," Jesse said.

"Attentive?" Dix said.

Jesse shrugged.

"I guess so," he said.

"Affectionate," Dix said.

"I imagine," Jesse said.

"But it was the wives who really struck you," Dix said.

"Yes."

"Jenn ever attentive and affectionate?" Dix said.

"Before we were married," Jesse said. "And a little while after."

"So she was capable of it," Dix said.

Jesse nodded.

"What made it so frustrating," he said. "She could and she didn't."

"Yes," Dix said. "That would be frustrating."

"And she was probably that way with other men?"

"Affectionate and attentive?" Dix said.

"Yeah."

"And you know this how?" Dix said.

"Figures," Jesse said. "She wanted something."

"How about these wives?" Dix said.

"They seem genuine to me," Jesse said.

"Perhaps you want them to be genuine," Dix said.

"Why?" Jesse said. "Why would I care?"

Dix looked at his watch. It was his signal that the fifty minutes were up.

"Don't know," Dix said. "Think about it. We can talk some more on Thursday."

"These two frogs get to marry the princesses," Jesse said. "I get the whore."

"We'll talk Thursday," Dix said.

HER SISTER let them into Roberta Moynihan's house and got them seated in the living room. When Roberta came in they all stood.

"I'm very sorry about your husband, Mrs. Moynihan," Jesse said. "We all are."

"Robbie," she said. "Please call me Robbie."

Jesse nodded. Robbie's face was pale and tight. But her eyes were dry. She seemed in control of herself. Rebecca Galen stood to the side, near her sister.

Jesse said, "This is Captain Healy, Robbie, the homicide commander for the state police. And the gentleman with him is Sergeant Liquori, of the state organized-crime unit."

Healy and Liquori nodded gravely.

"This is Roberta Moynihan," Jesse said.

Robbie smiled faintly and gestured toward the chairs they'd risen from.

"Please," she said, "sit down."

They sat.

"I know this will not be easy, Mrs. Moynihan," Healy said.

"Robbie," she said.

"But please put up with us as long as you can."

"I'll stay as long as you need, Captain," Robbie said. "It's the only way left for me to help my husband."

Her voice shook at the end of the sentence. But she breathed in, and when she spoke her voice was steady.

"What do you want to know?"

"Are you suspicious of anyone in your husband's death," Healy said.

"Francis had enemies," she said. "You know the life he used to lead."

Jesse saw Liquori's face twitch a little when Robbie said "used to lead," but he stayed quiet.

"Anyone specific?" Healy said.

"No, and nothing recent."

"No threats. No increased security?"

"No."

"Your husband carry a gun?"

"Sometimes," she said. "As I said, I know there were enemies."

"He wasn't wearing one when he was found," Healy said.

Robbie nodded.

"When's the last time you saw your husband?" Healy said.

"The night he was killed," Robbie said. "We had dinner and sat on the deck afterwards, as we usually do in good weather. . . ."

She paused and breathed and went on.

"And he said he was going for a walk. I offered to go with him, and he thanked me but said he needed to think a little and he'd do that better alone. . . . He said when we were together it was hard to think of anything else."

Healy nodded and looked at Liquori.

"If I may," Liquori said, "I'd like to read you a list of names, see if you recognize any."

"Of course," Robbie said.

Liquori read about ten names. Robbie listened attentively. When he was through she sat silently for a moment, then shook her head.

"I don't know any of them," she said. "I suppose they are acquaintances of my husband's?"

Liquori did not respond. He was a lean, bald guy with a big nose.

"Has your husband traveled lately?" he said.

"No," she said. "Francis hasn't gone anywhere at all for, like, a year."

Liquori nodded and looked at Healy. And so it went for maybe an hour while Jesse listened.

Finally Rebecca Galen stepped forward.

"I think we've talked long enough for today," she said. "I know my sister will be willing to talk again. But the doctor has prescribed a sedative, and I think she should take it."

"One other question," Jesse said. "Ray Mulligan? Where was he when Knocko was murdered?"

71

Robbie shook her head.

Rebecca said, "Knocko fired him the week before."

"They were old friends," Jesse said. "School days. Why'd he fire him?"

Robbie shook her head again.

"They had a disagreement," Rebecca said. "Neither of us knows about what. Our husbands' world was pretty much theirs."

"So, who does security now?" Jesse said.

"Bob," Rebecca said.

"Your Bob," Jesse said.

"Yes, he sort of looks after both estates."

"You know where Ray Mulligan is now?" Jesse said.

They both shook their heads.

"Robbie really needs to rest," Rebecca said.

"Sure," Jesse said, and stood.

Healy and Liquori stood as well. They said good-bye, and Rebecca showed them out.

As they went down the front walk to their car, Liquori said, "Never thought I'd see someone upset 'cause Knocko Moynihan died."

"Especially somebody like her," Jesse said.

"Especially," Liquori said.

THEY SAT in Healy's car, in the town beach parking lot. Liquori did most of the talking.

"I already gave Captain Healy the stuff I got on Reggie," Liquori said. "I assume he passed it on to you."

"He did," Jesse said.

"You got time to listen to background?" Liquori said.

Healy nodded. Jesse said, "Yes."

"Okay," Liquori said. "Him and Knocko had their problems."

"After Broz retired?" Healy said.

"Yeah," Liquori said.

He looked at Jesse.

"You wasn't around here twenty years ago."

"Nope."

"Guy named Broz ran pretty much the whole metropolitan area," Liquori said. "South almost to Providence, west to Springfield, north . . . hell, all the way to Montreal, for all I know."

"And when he quit there was a fight for territory," Jesse said.

"His kid wasn't up to it," Liquori said. "And there was some shouting and shooting and deal making, and we ended up with Gino Fish getting downtown, Tony Marcus got all the schwartzas, Knocko got the south, Reggie got north."

"When did this all happen?" Jesse said.

"Twenty years, give or take," Liquori said.

"'Bout the time Reggie married his wife," Jesse said.

"When did Knocko get married?" Healy said.

Liquori shrugged.

"I can check," he said. "Mighta had something to do with the deal they made?"

"Mighta," Jesse said.

"Like some of those old-time marriages," Liquori said. "You know? Like the king's sister marries the other king's brother or something."

"Maybe," Jesse said.

"What do we know about the wives?" Healy said.

"Nothing much," Liquori said. "They have never showed up on our screen, you know? No arrests, no accessory after charges. Nothing. Far as we know, they had nice marriages without any big troubles."

"At least no public ones," Healy said.

"None that we got," Liquori said.

"Any thoughts, Jesse?" Healy said.

"But far as I can tell, they were both happily married," Jesse said.

"Couple of fucking hooligans," Liquori said. "Like Knocko and Reggie?"

"Doesn't make sense to me, either," Jesse said. "Course, that may be because of the kind of marriage I had."

"Tell me about it," Liquori said.

"I been married forty-one years," Healy said. "Sometimes it works."

"And sometimes it don't," Liquori said.

Jesse didn't say anything. No one else did, either. The tide was out, and the smooth, wet expanse of beach that had been exposed by its going out ended in a line of seaweed and shells that marked its highest incursion. The sunlight was quick and right along the tops of the waves.

"Maybe we need to know more about these women," Healy said.

"I'll go through what I got," Liquori said.

"I can probably scrape up someone to look into them, too," Healy said.

Jesse nodded.

"No harm to it," he said. "Knocko actually retired?"

"No," Liquori said.

"Like Reggie is, partly."

"Healy told me Reggie still gets a skim on everything north," Jesse said.

"But that's about it, mostly passive. Not Knocko," Liquori said. "Knocko was still a player."

"Need the money?" Jesse said.

Healy shook his head. So did Liquori.

"Don't think so," Liquori said.

"Liked the power," Healy said.

"And the action," Liquori said.

"Don't we all," Jesse said. "You got any information on Ray Mulligan?"

"Probably," Liquori said.

"Lemme know what you got," Jesse said. "I'd like to talk with him."

"Because the firing was so convenient?" Liquori said.

"Yes," Jesse said.

Healy smiled.

"Especially for the shooter," he said.

20

JESSE WAS in his office, reading the file that Liquori had sent to him on Rebecca Galen and Roberta Moynihan. They were forty-one. They had gone to Paulus College. They had married their respective husbands in the same year, Rebecca in January, Roberta in May, in the same Catholic church. As far as could be determined, neither had been married before. There was no record of either of them ever holding a job. There were no children. Neither had a record. Jesse put the report down and leaned back in his chair. Nothing.

How had they spent their lives? *"Can I make you a martini, darling?" "What would you like for supper, dear?"*

He took in some air and let it out slowly.

Molly put her head in the doorway.

"The Patriarch guy from the Renewal is here reporting a missing person, Jesse," she said. "You want to see him?"

Jesse nodded. Molly disappeared and returned with the Patriarch. He took a seat in front of Jesse's desk.

"Coffee?" Jesse said.

The Patriarch shook his head and smiled slightly.

"We don't use caffeine," he said.

"I should have remembered," Jesse said.

"Perhaps you have other things to remember," the Patriarch said.

"And some I'd like to forget," Jesse said. "You have someone missing?"

"Cheryl DeMarco," he said. "She did not come home last night."

"You keep that close a tab?"

"We don't require them to come home," the Patriarch said. "But we need to know where they are, like any family."

"And you don't know."

"No. She went out yesterday to mingle and she didn't return."

" 'Mingle'?"

"We like all of us to mingle with our neighbors," the Patriarch said.

"Maybe some sort of romantic tryst?" Jesse said.

"Todd doesn't know where she is, either," the Patriarch said.

"Todd's her boyfriend?" Jesse said.

"Yes, her current life companion," the Patriarch said.

Jesse nodded.

"She wouldn't cheat on him," Jesse said.

"No."

"You're sure?"

"No," the Patriarch said. "Humans are too various for certainty. I don't believe she would cheat on her life companion."

"Have you tried her parents' home?"

"They will not take our calls," the Patriarch said.

"So as far as you know, they are not aware that she's missing?"

"I have no knowledge of them," the Patriarch said. "I know only that they hired a private detective to locate her and try to convince her to come home."

"Sunny Randall," Jesse said.

"You know her?"

"I do."

"Sometimes parents will arrange to have their children kidnapped," the Patriarch said. "Their own children."

"Not Sunny's style."

"No," the Patriarch said. "It didn't seem so to me, when we spoke."

"Have you told her that Cheryl is missing?" Jesse said.

"It didn't occur to me."

"I'll be speaking to her," Jesse said. "I'll tell her."

"You think she could be helpful?" the Patriarch said.

"She knows what Cheryl looks like," Jesse said. "And I don't."

"I hadn't thought of that."

"Do you have a picture?" Jesse said.

"No."

"How about Todd?"

"I don't know," the Patriarch said. "I can ask."

"She drive a car?" Jesse said.

"She didn't own one," the Patriarch said. "Why?"

"If she's got a license we can get a picture from the registry."

"Oh," the Patriarch said. "Of course. I am not very worldly about such things."

"No reason you should be," Jesse said.

"I can describe her," the Patriarch said.

"Sure," Jesse said.

The Patriarch described her. Jesse took a couple of notes.

When he finished describing, the Patriarch said, "Do you think she's all right?"

"Probably," Jesse said.

"Can you find her?"

"Probably," Jesse said.

THEY TOLD ME she'd been brainwashed by a cult," Sunny Randall said, "when they hired me."

She sat beside Jesse in the front seat of Jesse's car as they drove southbound on Route 128.

"And that they wanted me to find her and talk to her and, if possible, bring her home."

"So you went to visit," Jesse said.

"I did," Sunny said.

"And you found something less than Charles Manson and friends," Jesse said.

"You've talked with the Patriarch person?" Sunny said.

"Yes."

"The whole operation seems to me about as sinister as a Brownie troop," Sunny said.

"Less," Jesse said.

"You're right," Sunny said. "I never liked all that scouting crap, either."

"And the kid didn't want to leave," Jesse said.

"No."

"So I said maybe I could bring Mom and Dad," Sunny said. "And the kid laughed."

"But you tried," Jesse said.

"I did. I told them it seemed very unsinister, and maybe if they saw it . . ."

"What did they say?"

"They weren't interested. Their name isn't DeMarco, by the way. They changed it to Markham."

"Sounded more Concordian?" Jesse said.

"Yes. Elsa said DeMarco was too North End."

"But the kid is keeping her birth name," Jesse said.

"Guess so," Sunny said. "They'll never let me in, or you, either, if I'm with you. You don't have much official standing here."

"I've arranged for a Concord police detective to go with us, sort of disarm the matter of jurisdiction," Jesse said.

"No wonder you made chief," Sunny said.

"I made chief because the selectmen at the time wanted a drunk they could control," Jesse said.

"They erred," Sunny said.

"They got the drunk part right," Jesse said. "I guess they were a little off on the control part . . . so far."

"Well, aren't we down on ourselves today," Sunny said. "Want to share?"

Jesse didn't answer for a time. They reached Route 2 and turned west toward Concord.

"The night Knocko Moynihan got shot they couldn't find me. I was passed out dead drunk at home."

Sunny nodded.

"You know what set you off?" she said.

"Maybe I'm just a drunk," Jesse said.

"Whatever you are, Jesse," Sunny said, "you are not just a drunk."

Jesse shrugged.

"What's Dix say?"

"You think I told him?"

"Of course you told him," Sunny said. "What's he for?"

Jesse nodded slowly.

"We're working on that question," Jesse said.

" 'What he's for?' "

"No," Jesse said. "We're working on what set me off."

"Is it okay now," Sunny said. "I mean, in town?"

"Yes," Jesse said. "Molly and Suit covered for me. Said I was out of town at the time, an issue with my ex-wife."

"And the selectmen bought it?"

"They did," Jesse said. "They're not the smartest three guys in town."

"If they were," Sunny said, "they probably wouldn't be spending time as selectmen."

"Good point," Jesse said.

They paused behind several other cars at a stoplight at

the juncture with Route 2A's bypass, where Route 2 took a sharp turn southwest.

"But you must feel lousy about it," Sunny said.

"Yes."

"Ashamed," Sunny said.

"Yes."

"Had a drink since?" Sunny said.

"No."

"Miss it?"

Jesse nodded.

"Yes," he said.

"I don't think you're an alcoholic, Jesse," Sunny said. "I think you like to drink. I think when you're unhappy it helps you feel better. But I don't think you have to stop. I think you could drink in moderation if you get your, for lack of a better description, psyche settled."

The light changed. Jesse drove across the intersection and into Concord.

"I'll work on it," he said.

"I know you will," Sunny said.

They were quiet until they reached the Concord police station. Jesse pulled in and parked. Then he turned and put his hand on Sunny's thigh.

"Thank you," he said.

Sunny put her hand over his and smiled.

"You're welcome," she said.

THEY PICKED UP a Concord detective named Sherman Kennedy and drove in a Concord police car to the Markham home.

"It's ugly," Jesse said, as they got out of the cruiser. "But pretentious."

"True," Sunny said. "But it's much worse inside."

Kennedy laughed.

"Summers," he said, "I used to work construction while I was going to college. And I worked on this place. They built a whole bunch of them out here when mortgage money was easy."

He was a sturdy young guy with a crew cut and some modest lettering that said *Sherm* tattooed on his left wrist.

"Some foreclosures around here?"

"Like a damned going-out-of-business sale. People got balloon notes all of a sudden coming due. People who had no business buying one of these fucking monsters . . . 'Scuse me, Ms. Randall."

"My father was a cop," Sunny said. "I was a cop. I been hanging out with a bad element all my life."

Kennedy grinned.

"So you don't give a fuck," he said.

"I do not," Sunny said.

"Anyway," Kennedy said. "Lotta people bought places they couldn't afford with mortgages they shouldn't have gotten, or got places they couldn't afford but thought they could flip when the price went up, and the prices didn't go up and they couldn't carry the payments. . . . You know."

"I do," Sunny said.

They went to the front door. Kennedy put his badge folder in his breast pocket so that the badge showed. Elsa Markham answered the door.

"Hi," Kennedy said. "Detective Kennedy. I called earlier."

Elsa nodded. She looked at Sunny.

"Ms. Randall," she said.

"Mrs. Markham," Sunny said. "This is Jesse Stone. He's the chief of police in Paradise."

"Could you tell me what this is about?" Elsa said.

"May we come in?" Kennedy said.

"I am not required to let you in," she said, "unless you have some sort of document, I believe."

"True," Kennedy said. "But it would probably go easier if we came in."

"I'll decide that," Elsa said, "when I know what this is about."

"Your daughter is missing," Jesse said.

"I know that," Elsa said.

"She's missing from the Bond of the Renewal group home," Jesse said. "Where she lived, in Paradise."

Elsa was silent for a moment. Her face had a hard, sort of sick look, Jesse thought. As if she didn't feel well. Then she spoke.

"You could have informed me of that by a phone call," she said.

"We could," Jesse said.

"But you chose to come here," Elsa said.

"We did," Jesse said.

"Phone call's kind of cold," Kennedy said.

"They could have sent just you," she said to Kennedy. Then, turning back to Jesse: "Why did you and this woman come all the way out here?"

"Thought you might be helpful," Jesse said.

"I'm no longer responsible for her. She wants to shack up with some Jesus freak, I have no control over that."

"You think she's shacking up?" Jesse said.

"That would be her style," Elsa said.

"Any idea which Jesus freak?" Sunny said.

"None."

"Has she done this before?" Jesse said.

"What the hell do you think she's been doing in your stupid town for the last several months?" Elsa said.

"Any other instances," Jesse said, "besides her adventures in Paradise?"

"Drive through town," Elsa said. "Any long-haired, tattooed drug addict you see."

"Many of those in town?" Jesse asked Kennedy.

Kennedy grinned and covered up his *Sherm* tattoo with his right hand.

"Not that many," Kennedy said.

"Enough," Elsa said.

Kennedy shrugged.

"Is Mr. Markham here?" Jesse said.

"John's at work," she said. "As he is every other weekday."

"Industrious," Jesse said.

"It costs a lot of money to be Elsa and John Markham," she said.

"But worth it," Jesse said.

"Every penny," Elsa said.

"What does Mr. Markham do?" Sunny said.

"He's senior vice president of marketing at Pace Advertising," Elsa said.

"And Cheryl Markham?" Jesse said.

"She has chosen not to live under our roof," Elsa said. "She wants to be on her own. Very well. She is on her own."

"You've not heard from her," Jesse said.

"I have not."

"And you have no idea where she might be?" Jesse said.

"I do not."

"Or with whom?" Jesse said.

"None."

Jesse nodded. He looked at Sunny. She shrugged. He turned back to Elsa Markham.

He said, "Thank you for your time, Mrs. Markham."

She nodded and closed the door.

They walked back to the Concord patrol car. They got in. Kennedy started it up and let it idle.

Then he said, "Jesus Christ."

"You notice she didn't ask us to let her know if we found her daughter," Jesse said.

Sunny nodded.

"She don't care?" Kennedy said.

"Maybe she'll know if we find her daughter," Jesse said.

"How would she know . . ." Kennedy said, and paused halfway through the sentence. "Because she knows where the kid is."

"Might," Jesse said.

Sunny nodded.

"Which would mean she took the kid herself," Kennedy said.

"Or arranged it," Jesse said.

"You think they kidnapped their own daughter?" Kennedy said.

"People do," Jesse said.

"So, where is she?" Kennedy said.

"No way to know," Jesse said. "Yet."

"Why would they do it?" Kennedy said.

"For her own good?" Jesse said.

"Or," Sunny said, "because she's an embarrassment to them. Senior vice presidents have daughters at Wellesley."

"Or we could be wrong," Jesse said.

"We often are," Sunny said.

"Well," Kennedy said. "I'll talk to the chief, but I would guess the best we can do is keep an eye on the house some. Case she's there."

"And loose," Jesse said.

"You mean she might be locked up?"

"Might," Jesse said. "You know what she looks like?"

Kennedy shook his head.

"No," he said. "But I can probably get her picture from the high school."

"If you do," Jesse said, "send me a copy."

"Sure," Kennedy said. "Is there a license picture?"

"No."

"Parents don't have one?"

"They claim not," Sunny said.

"Shit," Kennedy said. "I got a hundred pictures of my daughter, and she's eleven months old."

"But not missing," Jesse said.

"Sometimes I wish she were," Kennedy said. "You got kids?"

Both Sunny and Jesse shook their heads.

"I wouldn'ta missed it," he said. "But it's hard on the wife."

Sunny and Jesse both nodded. Kennedy put the car in gear, and they drove out of the Markhams' driveway.

"Well," Kennedy said. "It could be worse. The house could have been foreclosed."

Jesse nodded.

"Yeah," he said. "That probably would have been worse."

23

JESSE SAT at his desk, reading the coroner's report on Knocko Moynihan. Cause of death was a nine-millimeter bullet in the back of the head. Like Ognowski. Except that Ognowski had been shot with a .22. Didn't mean they weren't related. Didn't mean they were. In fact, it didn't mean much of anything yet . . . except that they were both dead.

From the front of the station Jesse heard a door slam and Molly yelling "Hey!" and heavy footsteps. He opened the drawer in his desk where he kept his gun. A huge man in a blue suit came through his door. He barely fit. Jesse guessed six-six and probably three hundred pounds. The suit was a little small for him. Behind the man came a smallish woman with big blond hair. Her dress was flowered and puffy at the shoulders. It was very short. Behind both of them, as they pushed into the office, was Molly. She had her gun out and at her side, pointed at the floor.

"I don't know who this is, Jesse," she shouted from behind the big man. "He just pushed right past me and headed for your office."

Jesse nodded.

"Have a seat," he said.

The big man squeezed into one of Jesse's visitor chairs. The woman sat beside him, with her ankles crossed as modestly as possible given the skirt length. Her shoes were black with an ankle strap and a high cork platform. In the doorway, Molly still had her gun out, but she held it behind the doorjamb so it was not obvious.

The man said, "My name's Ognowski."

His voice seemed to come from someplace cavernous.

Jesse held up his hand.

"First," Jesse said. "Some rules."

"Rules?" the big man said.

"My name is Jesse Stone. I am the chief of police here. This is my station house."

"So?"

"In my station house you do what my officers, particularly this one"—he nodded at Molly—"tell you to do."

"This little girl?" the big man said.

"Her, me, whoever," Jesse said. "You understand that rule?"

"I go where I wish," the big man said.

"You go straight to a cell, you don't calm down," Jesse said.

The man stood slowly and looked down at Jesse.

"You will put me in a cell?"

Jesse took the gun from the drawer and pointed it at him.

"Yes," Jesse said. "We will shoot you if we have to."

The big man glanced back at Molly, who was also pointing her gun at him. Then he looked back at Jesse. He nodded once and sat back down. When he spoke, his voice had softened, but it continued to radiate power like a diesel generator.

"You are not welcoming," he said.

"Not yet," Jesse said.

The big man nodded again, as if in agreement with himself. Jesse put the gun back in the drawer, but he left the drawer open.

"You are a hard man," the big man said.

"Of course I am," Jesse said. "I'm the chief of police."

"I am a hard man, too," the big man said. "It is not a bad thing."

"Sometimes it is a good thing," Jesse said.

"My name is Nicolas Ognowski," the big man said. "I want to know who murdered my son."

"We don't know yet, Mr. Ognowski," Jesse said. "I'm sorry for your loss."

"When will you know?"

"As soon as we can," Jesse said. "Who is this?"

"Petrov's wife."

"And your name?" Jesse said.

"Natalya."

Her voice was small. Or maybe everyone's voice sounded small in the context of Ognowski's.

"My condolences, Mrs. Ognowski."

She bowed her head silently.

"We have very little evidence yet regarding the death of Petrov Ognowski," Jesse said. "Do either of you have anything to tell me?"

"She does," Ognowski said.

Natalya continued to look down at her lap, which was barely covered by her skirt.

"Do you know something useful, Mrs. Ognowski?" Jesse said.

She nodded. Jesse nodded toward the door where Molly still stood, her gun still out and hidden by the doorjamb.

"Would you prefer to talk to Molly?" Jesse said.

"She'll talk to you," Ognowski said. "Tell him now, Natalya."

She blushed.

"Another woman," Natalya said.

"Do you know who?" Jesse said.

Natalya shook her head.

"Are you sure?" Jesse said.

Natalya nodded.

"Did you ever see her?" Jesse said.

Natalya shook her head.

"Did he tell you about her?"

She shook her head again.

"But you are sure he was seeing another woman," Jesse said.

She nodded her head vigorously.

"How did you know?" Jesse said.

She didn't answer.

"Tell him how you know, Natalya," Ognowski said.

Natalya raised her eyes and looked straight at Jesse. Her face was red.

"I am with him at night," she said. "We are doing love. And I am knowing I am not first person he do this with today."

"How do you know?" Jesse said.

"I know. I know like a voice saying in my head, he do this already today. I know."

She looked hard at Jesse.

"You understand?" she said.

It seemed to matter to her that he did. He thought of how he had known that with Jenn. He did understand. He nodded slowly.

"Yes," he said. "I do."

She smiled faintly.

"Did it happen more than once?" Jesse said.

"Many," Natalya said.

"But you don't know who?"

"No."

"Could it have been more than one?" Jesse said.

Natalya looked at Nicolas Ognowski.

"Petrov liked women," Ognowski said.

"Doesn't mean it got him killed," Jesse said.

"It is a clue," Ognowski said. "More than you had before we came."

"True," Jesse said.

"You will find him," Ognowski said. "Or I will. If I do, it will save you much trouble."

"And if I warned you to stay out of it?" Jesse said.

Ognowski stared silently at Jesse.

Then he said, "Petrov was my only son."

Jesse nodded.

"Anything else you can tell me?" he said.

"That is all we know," Ognowski said.

"Where can I get in touch with you?" Jesse said.

"I will get in touch with you," Ognowski said.

He stood. Natalya stood as soon as he did.

"You would not let me walk over you," Ognowski said.

"No," Jesse said.

"Many people do."

"You have a lot of presence," Jesse said.

Ognowski nodded.

"It is a good sign that you would not," he said.

When he left, Jesse walked to the front of the station with him and stood in the front door of the station and watched them get into a waiting cab. As it pulled away, Jesse took down the hack number of the cab. Then he looked at Molly.

"Jesus Christ," Molly said, and holstered her gun.

24

I T'S FUNNY," Sunny said to Dr. Silverman, as they sat in
Dr. Silverman's office. "I have such conflicting emotions when
I come to see you."

Dr. Silverman nodded almost imperceptibly. It was one of
her nondirective "let's talk about that" signs.

"I mean, I'm hoping to get well," Sunny said. "And I'm
eager to find out more about myself. But I also hate to have to
face some of what I find out. And I hate to have to admit it to
you."

Dr. Silverman nodded and waited.

"But besides all of those kinds of conflicting emotions,"
Sunny said, "I am always eager to see what you're wearing."

Dr. Silverman tilted her head and raised her eyebrows. It was her "tell me about that" sign.

"You are beautiful, of course," Sunny said. "But you are also the most perfectly pulled-together woman I've ever seen."

"'Pulled together,'" Dr. Silverman said.

Well, Sunny thought, *she remains calm in the face of praise.*

"I mean, everything fits, and everything matches, and everything is appropriate," Sunny said. "It's not just pulled together. It's . . . You're very complete."

Dr. Silverman nodded and waited again.

"Or is all of that just transference?" Sunny said.

Dr. Silverman smiled.

"I hope not," she said.

Sunny laughed.

"It's not like I run around gushing to women friends about how complete they seem."

"'Complete,'" Dr. Silverman said.

"You know, everything works. Competent. Contained. In control. The way you look is like a . . . like a symbol of how you are."

Dr. Silverman nodded. Sunny was quiet.

After a time, Dr. Silverman said, "Of course, you have no way of knowing how I am."

Sunny stared at her.

"Well," Sunny said, after a while. "I see you twice a week, and have for some time now."

"And what do we always talk about?" Dr. Silverman said.

Sunny was silent for a moment. Then she smiled slightly.

"Me," Sunny said.

Dr. Silverman nodded.

"So why have I constructed this whole portrait of you based basically on how you look."

"It might be interesting to know," Dr. Silverman said.

They sat quietly.

"Well, you are attractive," Sunny said. "And you're accomplished—you know, Harvard Ph.D. psychotherapist. Successful relationship?"

Dr. Silverman didn't answer.

"Of course," Sunny said. "It's about me, not you."

Dr. Silverman made a faint assenting movement with her head. Sunny sat back a little in her chair and looked at the ceiling while she thought.

"So why do I need you to be the woman I described?"

More silence. Then Dr. Silverman broke it.

"Do you know any women like the one you've described?" Dr. Silverman said.

"No," Sunny said. "Not really."

"Do you know anyone like that?" Dr. Silverman said. "Male or female?"

"My father," Sunny said. "And . . . I guess my ex-husband."

There was more quiet.

"My father," Sunny said. "And my ex-husband. There must be something pretty shrinky there."

Dr. Silverman nodded without exactly agreeing. Sunny never quite knew how she stayed so noncommittal.

"Are you that woman?" Dr. Silverman said.

"Me?"

Dr. Silverman nodded.

"God, no," Sunny said.

"Would you like to be that woman?" Dr. Silverman said.

Sunny looked at the ceiling some more. Then she lowered her eyes and looked at Dr. Silverman.

"Aha!" she said.

TALKED to the cab company," Molly told Jesse. "They said the cabbie picked up Mr. Ognowski and his daughter-in-law in front of the Four Seasons Hotel in Boston, took them here, then back to the Four Seasons."

Jesse nodded.

"I called the hotel, and Ognowski's not registered there."

"Call around," Jesse said.

"Could be there under another name," Molly said.

Jesse nodded.

"Or he could be elsewhere and picked up a cab there because it was handy, or to confuse us."

Jesse nodded.

"I'll call around," Molly said.

"Good idea," Jesse said.

Molly started to leave. Then she stopped and closed the door and turned back to Jesse.

"How are you?" she said.

"That's not entirely clear," Jesse said.

"You talk to that shrink?"

"Dix," Jesse said. "Yes."

"What does he say?"

"He nods and says, 'Um-hm.'"

"Which means?" Molly said.

Jesse smiled.

"I think it means, 'We'll talk about it some more,'" Jesse said.

"You believe in that stuff?" Molly said.

"Shrinkage?" Jesse said. "I'm hopeful."

"You think it's helped you?"

"I'm better than I was," Jesse said.

Molly nodded.

"Ever hear from your ex?" Molly said.

"No."

Molly was silent for a moment. Jesse waited.

"How about you and Sunny," Molly said.

"We're fine," Jesse said.

"What's 'fine' mean?" Molly said.

"Means I don't want to talk about it."

Molly nodded.

"That's what I thought it meant," she said. "Sunny's a nice woman."

"So are you," Jesse said.

Molly smiled.

"True," she said. "But I'm married."

"And Sunny isn't," Jesse said.

"Exactly."

"She's divorced," Jesse said. "But she's not out of it yet."

"And you are?"

"Yes."

"Which," Molly said, "is why you drank yourself into a coma last week?"

"That was regret," Jesse said. "I am done with Jenn."

Molly nodded.

"I appreciate what you did to cover for me while I was in the coma," Jesse said.

"Suit, too," Molly said.

"I know," Jesse said. "You went further out on a limb for me than you had any good reason to."

"You're a good cop, Jesse. We didn't want one excess to end your career."

"There's been more than one," Jesse said. "But I thank you. Being a cop is what I've got right now."

"You have us," Molly said.

" 'Us'? "

"The Paradise police department, all of us, like your family."

"Some family," Jesse said.

"Just remember that we love you, Jesse," Molly said. "All of us."

"You, too?" Jesse said.

"Me especially," Molly said.

"Does that mean that you and I could. . . ?"

"No," Molly said. "It doesn't."

She grinned at him.

"But you could maybe promote me to sergeant instead," Molly said. "You know, as a gesture of gratitude?"

"Absolutely not," Jesse said.

Molly sighed loudly and spoke.

"Maybe I should have said yes."

26

THEY WERE on the Southeast Expressway, with Suit driving.

"Why are we going to Hempstead?" Suit said.

"See what we can find out about Rebecca and Roberta Bangston," Jesse said.

"They're from Hempstead?"

"Yep."

"Who we gonna talk with?" Suit said.

"Start with the Hempstead chief of police."

"Wow," Suit said. "Two in the same room. What am I doing there?"

Jesse grinned.

"We may need coffee," he said.

Suit nodded.

"It's good to be useful," he said.

Hempstead was the most affluent town in the southern commuter suburbs. The police station was white clapboard with green shutters.

"Slick," Suit said, as he got out of the car.

"What's wrong with red brick?" Jesse said.

"You see an awful lot of it," Suit said.

"I suppose," Jesse said.

The chief's office was big. It had a big desk, and a big American flag, and big windows, which overlooked a golf course. The chief was dark-haired and overweight, but his uniform was tailored to fit.

"Howard Parrott," he said, when Jesse came in.

"Jesse Stone," Jesse said. "And Luther Simpson."

They all shook hands.

"We're down here looking into a couple of former residents," Jesse said. "Twins, who, when they lived here, were Roberta and Rebecca Bangston."

"The Bangstons are a well-known family here," Parrott said.

"You know them?"

"I knew Mr. and Mrs. Bangston," Parrott said. "Had a big place on the water. Had a huge picnic every year, raised a lot of money for Catholic charities."

"The twins would be about forty-one," Jesse said.

"So they graduated high school in 1986," Parrott said.

He grinned.

"I'm not that quick at math," he said. "One of my nephews

graduated that year. My sister's kid. I was a patrolman then, kids had a huge beer party, and we had to break it up. I hadn't been there, he'da been tossed in the clink."

"What's an uncle for," Jesse said.

"You got that right," Parrott said. "To serve and protect, and get your nephew off."

Parrott grinned again and leaned back in his chair.

"Now he's a cop, too," Parrott said. "Works for me."

"Probably grateful," Jesse said.

"Sure," Parrott said. "He was a kid, you know. You guys ever drink too much?"

Suit nodded.

Jesse said, "Now and then."

"Sure," Parrott said. "Me, too. Why are you interested in the Bangston girls?"

"Roberta's husband was murdered," Jesse said.

"Really? What a shame. You suspect the girls?"

"Nope."

"So why you down here talking about them," Parrott said.

"Got nowhere else to be," Jesse said.

"That's police work for you," Parrott said, "isn't it?"

"Gotta start somewhere," Jesse said.

"Lemme make a suggestion," Parrott said. "I got a Rotary meeting at noon, but my nephew is here; why don't I turn you over to him. I'll bet he even knows these girls."

"Go to high school with them?" Jesse said.

"No," Parrott said. "He went to Hempstead High. Bangstons woulda sent their kids to Holy Spirit."

"Catholic school," Jesse said.

"Yeah. But the schools are close and the kids mix with each other," Parrott said.

He leaned forward and flipped a switch on the intercom.

"Sergeant Mike Mayo, please come to the chief's office," Parrott said.

27

MAYO WAS obviously a weight lifter, a big genial-looking guy with short red hair and a nineteen-inch neck. He shook hands with Jesse and Suit when they were introduced.

"Mikey," Parrott said. "These people are interested in the Bangston twins; you know them?"

Mayo smiled.

"I do," he said.

"Could you talk to Jesse and Luther about them?" Parrott said. "I gotta go to Rotary."

"Sure," Mayo said.

"Use my office," Parrott said. "Close the door when you're through."

Parrott shook hands with Jesse and Suitcase and left. Mayo went around and sat behind Parrott's desk.

"Try it out for size," he said.

"I notice you smiled when Chief Parrott asked if you knew the Bangston twins."

Mayo nodded.

"Tell me why you want to know about them," Mayo said.

Jesse told him.

"Living side by side," Mayo said.

"Uh-huh."

Mayo shook his head and smiled again.

"I knew them," he said. "We all knew them. We went to Hempstead, they went to Spirit. But we still hung together. We all believed that Spirit girls were easy. . . . You know how it was in high school."

"Ever hopeful," Jesse said.

Mayo nodded.

"We used to call them the Bang Bang Twins."

"Because they were, in fact, easy?" Jesse said.

"Yes."

"None of my business," Jesse said. "But did you . . . ?"

"Most of us did," Mayo said. "But they had a trick they did."

"Trick," Jesse said.

"You never knew which one you were having sex with."

"On purpose?" Jesse said.

"Yeah, they used to like to switch so one time you'd be with one of them, and next time you would think you were with her and you were with her sister."

"How'd you know?" Suit said.

"When it was over, they'd tell you," Mayo said. "Sometimes they'd take turns with you and make you guess who was who."

"Guess they didn't take all that Catholic stuff too serious," Suit said.

"Their parents did," Mayo said.

"They were famous for this twin sex trick?" Jesse said.

"Yeah, the Bang Bang Twins."

"I wonder why they did it," Jesse said.

"They liked it, I guess," Mayo said. "They were always into the twin thing, you know. I mean, a lot of twins dress different, do their hair different, maybe, different makeup. I mean, they don't want to be exactly the same."

"The Bang Bangs did?" Jesse said.

"They wanted to be identical," Mayo said. "When we were in grammar school they always came to school in the same outfits, same hair, everything."

"So their mother probably wanted them to look alike," Jesse said.

"I guess."

"Know the parents?"

"Not really. Old man was a contractor. He's dead now. They got a lot of money. Big house on the water. Big into church stuff. Probably guilt."

"About what?" Jesse said.

"Old man was always kind of a sleaze. Never got convicted. But a lotta talk about not meeting the specs for his construction deals. Lotta talk about sweetheart deals with the state. Stuff like that. Lotta people say he fooled around."

"How'd he die?" Jesse said.

"Heart attack," Mayo said. "On a business trip to Cleveland. I think he was in the saddle at the time."

"How about the mother?" Jesse said.

"Mother's still around."

"Can you take us over there?" Jesse said.

"Sure," Mayo said.

28

MRS. BANGSTON WAS a brusque woman, not tall but erect. Her hair was iron-gray. She had pince-nez glasses, and she reminded Jesse of his elementary-school principal. They sat in the living room of her big glass-fronted modern home looking out over Hempstead Bay. It seemed totally out of keeping with the white-clapboard/weathered-shingle look of the town. It was out of keeping with the furnishings as well, which were overstuffed Victorian everywhere that Jesse could see. It was as if her husband had built the outside and she had furnished the inside without regard to each other.

"I did not know that Roberta's husband had died," she said. "I am sorry to hear it, and sorrier still that he was murdered."

"No one told you?" Jesse said.

"No."

"Perhaps they wanted to spare you," Jesse said.

"My girls call every Christmas and Easter," Mrs. Bangston said. "I get flowers every Mother's Day. I forward their mail."

"After all these years?" Jesse said.

"Yes, they still get mail here."

"Do you see much of them?" Jesse said.

"Not very much," she said. "They are dutiful, but nothing more."

"Do you know their husbands?"

"I have never met either," Mrs. Bangston said.

"Not even at the weddings?" Jesse said.

"No."

There were some rosary beads on the coffee table in front of where she sat. She looked at them.

"You weren't at the weddings?" Jesse said.

"No."

"Either wedding," Jesse said.

"No."

"Were you invited?" Jesse said.

"Yes."

"But?"

"I did not approve of the men they were marrying," Mrs. Bangston said.

"What did you disapprove of?" Jesse said.

"They were both criminals," Mrs. Bangston said.

"How did you know that?" Jesse said.

"My husband told me."

"He knew these men?"

"I don't know," Mrs. Bangston said. "My husband knew a great many people. Business was his sphere; mine was home and family."

"Your husband did business with the men your daughters married?"

"I don't know."

"Do you know how they met their husbands?"

"I do not," she said.

She leaned forward and picked up her rosary beads from the coffee table and held them in her left hand.

"They had the finest religious education we could give them. Holy Spirit High School. Paulus College. They made their First Communion side by side in identical white dresses. They were confirmed together . . . and they married criminals."

"The Church is important to you," Jesse said.

Jesse had no idea where he was going. But he wanted to keep her talking.

"It has been the center of my life," she said. "My late husband and I attended Mass every Sunday. Since he has gone, I attend every morning. It is my consolation."

"The girls are the most identical twins I've ever seen," Jesse said.

"Yes. Even I cannot always distinguish them."

"They dress alike," Jesse said. "They do their hair alike. Makeup, manner, everything."

"Yes."

"Did you encourage them in that?" Jesse said.

"Of course; had God not wanted them to remain identical, he would not have created them identical."

"Did your husband feel that way, too?" Jesse said.

She smiled and looked past Jesse out the wide front window at the whitecaps in the bay.

"My husband used to say he was luckier than other fathers. He had the same daughter twice."

The room was quiet. Mayo was sitting a little behind Jesse with his arms folded. Suit sat beside Jesse with his hands folded in his lap.

"You got any questions, Suit?" Jesse said.

Suit looked startled. Jesse waited.

"Were your daughters good girls?" he said finally.

"They were angels when they were small. As adults they have disappointed me," Mrs. Bangston said.

"Anything besides marrying men you disapproved of?" Suit said.

"No," Mrs. Bangston said.

Suit looked at Jesse.

"Anything at all," Jesse said, "that you can think of that might aid us in our investigation?"

"No."

The room was silent. Mrs. Bangston continued to look past them at the ocean. It was as if she'd left them. The beads moved in her left hand, and Jesse realized she was praying. He stood.

"Thank you for your time, Mrs. Bangston," he said.

She nodded slightly and continued to move the beads slowly with her left hand.

"We'll find our way out," Jesse said.

Again, a slight nod.

The three cops left.

29

T HE BANG BANG TWINS," Suit said, as they drove back up Route 3 toward Boston.

"Yep."

"Wish we'd had them when I was in high school," Suit said.

"Luck of the draw," Jesse said.

"You said those sisters were so nice," Suit said.

"I did," Jesse said.

"And you didn't know the half of it," Suit said.

Jesse nodded.

"I think we need to find out if they are still the Bang Bang Twins."

"Want me to see what I can learn?" Suit said.

"I do," Jesse said. "You grew up in this town. They've lived here awhile. Maybe you know some of the same people."

"I don't know any people like that," Suit said.

"Maybe Hasty Hathaway's wife?" Jesse said.

Suit's face turned red.

"Man, you don't forget nothing," he said.

"Of course not," Jesse said. "I'm the chief of police."

"Mother was kind of weird," Suit said.

"She's religious," Jesse said.

"Like I said."

"It works for some people," Jesse said.

"Not for the Bang Bang Twins," Suit said.

"So young, so judgmental," Jesse said.

"What? You think what they do is okay?"

Jesse shrugged.

"You think Mrs. Bangston knows about the Bang Bang stuff?" Suit said.

"Yes."

"Because she sort of clammed up when you asked her about why she was disappointed in them?"

"Uh-huh."

"See," Suit said. "I notice stuff."

"You do," Jesse said. "There's a donut place at this next exit."

"You notice stuff, too," Suit said, and turned into the exit.

They sat in the car in the parking lot and had donuts and coffee.

"All-American grub," Suit said.

"Highly nutritious," Jesse said. "I wonder how the father knew Knocko and Reggie were bad guys."

Suit swallowed some donut and drank coffee.

"Maybe they done some business or something," Suit said. "Mike says the old man was kind of shady."

"Be good to know," Jesse said.

"Why?"

"Because we don't know," Jesse said.

"That's what you always say."

"Except when we do know," Jesse said.

"Except then," Suit said. "Is any of this going to solve our two murders?"

"Maybe," Jesse said.

"Or maybe not?"

"Or maybe not," Jesse said.

"I guess we should look into that, too," Suit said.

"I'll do that," Jesse said. "You work on the Bang Bang Twins."

"So, why'd you drag me along all the way down to Hempstead?"

"Training," Jesse said.

"So I could become a crack sleuth like you?"

"Observe and learn," Jesse said.

"I do," Suit said. "I've already picked up the vocabulary. Maybe. Might. Possibly. I don't know."

"If Paradise ever gets a slot for detectives, you'll be the first appointed," Jesse said.

Suit grinned.

"Maybe," he said.

THE MARKHAMS LIVED at the head of a circle off a street
that ran from downtown Concord out toward Route 2. Sunny
parked her car across the street from the circle and maybe fifty
yards up the street. It was her second week. Her cell phone
rang. It was Jesse.

"Oh, good," Sunny said. "I'm so bored I'm close to fainting."

"What are you doing?" Jesse said.

"Sitting in my car doing surveillance on Mrs. Markham."

"Cheryl DeMarco's mother?"

"Yep."

"Can't let it go, huh?" Jesse said.

"Nope," Sunny said. "I'm worried about the kid."

"Anything so far?"

"Mrs. Markham takes yoga, and she shops for food," Sunny said.

"Of course, she may not know where her daughter is," Jesse said.

"Possible," Sunny said.

"Could Cheryl be in the house?" Jesse said.

"I don't think so," Sunny said. "They're the kind of people would send her somewhere."

"Who would they send her with?"

"When they first hired me they asked if I knew someone who would kidnap her."

"So it is not beyond their thinking," Jesse said.

"No."

"Somebody had to encounter her," Jesse said, "and persuade her to go with them to a place, and the place would need to persuade her to stay there."

"Yes," Sunny said.

"Who would that be?"

"I don't know," Sunny said. "But maybe I can find out."

"You got a plan?"

"Not everyone will coerce a young woman into a place she doesn't want to go," Sunny said. "Even at the behest of her parents."

"True," Jesse said.

"And," Sunny said, "they don't seem like people who'd know someone who would."

"No, they don't."

"Unless it was a lawyer," Sunny said.

"The right kind of lawyer," Jesse said.

"Their lawyer might know the right kind of lawyer."

"Or they might just have a friend who's a lawyer," Jesse said.

"If he went to an Ivy League law school," Sunny said.

"You might try checking that out," Jesse said.

"It's all hypothesis and supposition and guessing," Sunny said.

"That's called detection," Jesse said.

"But will it be as much fun as sitting in my car in Concord," Sunny said, "watching people dressed funny ride their bicycles?"

"Hard to imagine that it could be more fun than that," Jesse said.

"But it seems worth a try," Sunny said. "Did you call just to talk about me and my case?"

"Actually, I called to talk about me and my case," Jesse said. "But I got sidetracked."

"By me and my case," Sunny said.

"Exactly."

"So, how are you," Sunny said. "How's your case."

"The time I told you about, when I went on a bender and Molly and Suit covered for me."

"Yes," Sunny said.

"One of the things that set me off was I met these women married to a couple of mobsters, who seemed perfect wives," Jesse said.

"And you went into a tailspin," Sunny said. "Why them and not me?"

"Yes," Jesse said. "You know about that kind of tailspin?"

"Yes."

"Present company excluded," Jesse said, "these are two of the most compelling women I ever met. They're identical twins. In high school they were known as the Bang Bang Twins."

"They were promiscuous," Sunny said.

"They used to switch off on the same guy, see if he could tell which was which."

"Wow," Sunny said. "They ever have sex in the dressing room of an upscale boutique in Beverly Hills?"

"Maybe at the same time," Jesse said.

"Tell me more," Sunny said.

Jesse did. When he finished, Sunny was silent for a moment. Then she said, "Doesn't mean they haven't matured into lovely women."

"Unless they're still doing the Bang Bang thing."

"Whatever else it is," Sunny said, "it would provide several swell motives for murder."

"It would."

"And they each live with a husband, side by side," Sunny said.

"True."

"Does what you learned about them make you uncomfortable with your appraisal of women."

"And wives," Jesse said.

"Even worse," Sunny said.

"Much," Jesse said.

"Dix have any insights?" Sunny said.

"Haven't seen him yet," Jesse said. "First I need to know what the Bang Bang Twins are like these days."

"But you've talked about your first reaction to them," Sunny said.

"Yes."

"He say anything interesting?"

"No, but he looked interested," Jesse said.

"It's a start," Sunny said.

Again, they were quiet on their respective cell phones.

"You want to have dinner?" Jesse said.

"Tonight?"

"Yes."

"I'll come there," Sunny said.

"Really?" Jesse said. "Long drive home at night."

"Maybe I'll bring a little suitcase," Sunny said.

"What a very good idea," Jesse said.

"Don't get your hopes up," Sunny said.

"My hopes are always up," Jesse said.

"Good to know," Sunny said.

"Either way," Jesse said, "it'll be nice to see you."

"Either way?"

"Either way."

Again, they were quiet.

Then Sunny said, "Gray Gull?"

"Seven o'clock," Jesse said.

31

FRESHLY SHOWERED and sitting alone in Jesse's living room, wearing one of Jesse's shirts for a bathrobe, Sunny called Pace Advertising and asked for John Markham.

"Mr. Markham is in Chicago this week. May I transfer you to his voice mail?"

"No," Sunny said. "Do you have an attorney on staff?"

"That would be Mr. Cahill. May I connect you?"

"Yes," Sunny said. "Thank you."

The line went silent, then a phone picked up and a male voice said, "Don Cahill."

"Hi, Mr. Cahill," Sunny said. "This is Sonya Stone in John Markham's office. He's out of town, and I need a little favor."

"Whaddya need, Sonya?"

"Mr. Markham asked me to call that lawyer you sent him to, and I've lost his name and number."

"John won't like that," Cahill said.

"I know," Sunny said. "Can you save me?"

Cahill laughed.

"Cahill to the rescue," he said. "Wait a second."

Sunny waited. Cahill came back.

"Harry Lyle," he said, and recited the phone number.

"Thank you," Sunny said. "You're an angel."

"You better believe it, Sonya," Cahill said. "You can stop by anytime to thank me."

"I will," Sunny said, and hung up.

She looked at Ozzie Smith's picture on the wall behind the bar.

"Sometimes, Ozzie," she said out loud, "I dazzle myself."

She went into the bedroom and dressed and made the bed. The picture of Jenn that used to be on the bedside table was gone. Sunny smiled to herself as she packed her small suitcase.

Sonya Stone?

She cleaned up the breakfast dishes. It was kind of fun being housewifely. When she was through she went back in the living room and got out a copy of the Boston phone book and looked up Harry Lyle. He was listed as a criminal lawyer. She phoned and made an appointment, calling herself Rose Painter. Then she went into the kitchen where Jesse kept a notepad, and sat at the kitchen table and wrote him a note and left it on the bed pillow.

I'm glad I brought my little suitcase.

XXOO

S

As she drove back toward Boston, she thought about Jesse. She liked having sex with him. What was not to like . . . as a sex partner. As a life partner? There was the drinking problem and the ex-wife. Sunny wasn't sure that he had actually rid himself of Jenn and the way he felt about Jenn.

She gave a small humorless laugh.

Like I'm rid of Richie. What kind of prospect am I for Jesse? I don't have a drinking problem, but I very well may be more addicted to my ex than he has been to his. Are we both settling for second best? Dr. Silverman had said once that she was using other men as an anodyne. Were she and Jesse doing that, killing their pain with each other? . . . *Worse ways, I suppose.*

32

CHARLIE TRAXAL," Rita Fiore said, "Jesse Stone."
Jesse shook hands with Traxal.

"Charlie's the chief investigator for the Norfolk County DA,"
Rita said. "Jesse's the chief of police in Paradise."

"Any friend of Rita's," Traxal said.

"Covers a lot of ground," Rita said.

They were having lunch at Locke-Ober.

"Rita tells me you used to be in L.A.," Traxal said to Jesse.

"Robbery homicide," Jesse said.

"So you done some street work," Traxal said.

"Yep."

"Charlie often worked with me when I was a prosecutor

down there," Rita said. "He knows more about crime south of Boston than anyone I've ever met."

"Rita knew a lot herself," Traxal said. "Until she went upscale to the big, fancy law firm."

"Which is paying for your lunch," Rita said.

"Thing I like best about big, fancy law firms," Traxal said. "I think I'll have the Lobster Savannah."

"Jesse is looking for South Shore crime gossip," Rita said.

Traxal looked at Jesse.

"You've come to the right place," he said. "Whaddya need?"

"Neal Bangston," Jesse said. "Knocko Moynihan, Reggie Galen."

Traxal leaned back and drank some of his iced tea. He was a sturdy-looking man, with gray hair and horn-rimmed glasses.

"I never got the bastard," he said.

"Which one?" Jesse said.

"Any of them, but I wanted Bangston most."

"Why?"

"Because we never caught him. Moynihan and Galen both did time, but Bangston." Traxal shook his head. "Lord Bangston of Hempstead."

"Dirty?"

"Absolutely," Traxal said.

"Couldn't prove it?"

"Never."

"He connected to Knocko and Reggie?" Jesse said.

"Yes."

"Tell me about it," Jesse said.

"You want stuff I can prove?" Traxal said.

"Tell me what you know," Jesse said.

"Bangston was a construction guy," Traxal said. "Knocko used to work for him once, bricklayer. Knocko was a tough guy. Used to box, strong as hell. Had a reputation, you know? And when there was trouble with somebody who didn't like the work Bangston was doing or the wages he was paying, he took to sending Knocko around to discuss it. And the bigger Bangston Construction got, the more there was to discuss."

"Like?"

"Construction not up to code, nonunion labor, pay below minimum, illegal immigrants, lot of overcharges."

"So," Jesse said, "Knocko became more and more important."

"And so did Bangston," Traxal said. "Big man in Hempstead. Big man in the Church, had a big charity event every year on his lawn. Married some rich Catholic broad from an important family. Moved up in the world."

Rita sat quietly, listening to them talk. Nearly everyone who came into the restaurant, Jesse noticed, looked at her.

"Meanwhile, Knocko started freelancing and got himself busted for extortion," Traxal said. "Three years in Garrison."

"Where he meets Reggie Galen," Jesse said.

"Soul mates," Traxal said.

He looked at Rita.

"You miss all this stuff, babe?" Traxal said.

"Everything but the thirty-thousand-dollar salary," she said.

"Anyway, after both of them get out of jail, Bangston is trying to expand on the North Shore, and he's having some trouble with Reggie Galen, who's charging Bangston a security fee for everything that he does up there. So Bangston gets hold of Knocko and tells him the problem, and Knocko says, 'I know the guy,' and pretty soon they're all thick as thieves."

"Lemme guess," Jesse said. "Reggie's the North Shore Knocko."

"And everyone's making money."

"You know Bangston's twin daughters married his two thugs?" Jesse said.

Traxal nodded. Rita whistled softly.

"Yeah," he said. "I don't think Bangston liked that much, but by now it's not clear if Knocko and Reggie work for Bangston or he works for them."

"You been accumulating evidence for a long time," Jesse said.

"Looked at a lot of paper," Traxal said. "Talked to a lot of people."

"None of whom will talk on the record."

"Nope."

"Without which the paper's no good."

"Nope."

"Careful guys," Jesse said.

"And smart," Traxal said. "You're interested because of Knocko getting aced in your town."

"Yep."

"Pretty thorough guy," Traxal said.

"I am," Jesse said. "Guy worked for Reggie Galen got whacked, too."

"Connected?"

"Seems likely," Jesse said.

"Two thugs?" Rita said. "In the same month? In a town like Paradise? I'd say it seems very likely."

"Sure," Traxal said. "What did this guy do for Reggie?"

"Slugger," Jesse said.

"Suspects?"

"Not really."

"Think one of the Bangston girls might have been involved?" Traxal said.

"Don't know," Jesse said.

"You asked about them."

"I ask about everything," Jesse said. "You know anything about their reputation?"

Traxal smiled.

"The Bang Bang Twins?" he said.

"I guess you do," Jesse said.

"But I don't," Rita said. "And I want to hear about it. The Bang Bang Twins?"

They told her. When they were through, Rita sat quietly for a moment.

Then she said, "I wish I had a twin."

33

HARRY LYLE WAS a tall, portly man with receding hair and a good tan. He wore a blue pin-striped double-breasted suit and a white shirt with a white silk tie. He watched closely as Sunny sat down and crossed her legs.

Good sign, Sunny thought.

"How can I help you, Ms. Painter," he said.

"Mrs. Painter," Sunny said. "Mrs. Elwood Painter."

Lyle nodded.

"Very well," he said. "Mrs. Painter, how may I help?"

"I . . . It's my son."

He nodded kindly.

"What about your son?" he said.

"He's left home."

"Oh?"

"He's joined a cult," Sunny said. "I want him out of it."

"Kids, huh?" Lyle said. "How old is he?"

"Eighteen."

"Okay."

"He's not old enough to be on his own with a bunch of Bible-thumpers," Sunny said.

"I'm sure you're right," Lyle said.

"Can you help me?" Sunny said. "Can we get a court order or something?"

"Might take some doing, at his age," Lyle said. "How did you happen to come to me?"

"A friend," Sunny said. "Of a friend."

"They have names?"

Sunny shook her head.

"They told me that you had experience with adolescent rebellion, and they made me promise not to tell anyone they'd told me." Sunny smiled and leaned forward and lowered her voice a little. "I think they don't want anyone to know that they had problems with their children."

"People often don't," Lyle said. "Everyone has problems. No need to be ashamed."

"I know," Sunny said. "But I promised."

"Well, arrangements for something like this," Lyle said, "can be expensive."

"Money is not a problem," Sunny said. "Elwood has a great deal of money."

"If there's enough," Lyle said, "it's possible to arrange something."

"Can you take him away from these people?" Sunny said.

"It might be arranged," Lyle said.

"If you did, how would we keep him from going back?" Sunny said. "We can't just lock him in his room."

"There's a residential treatment center in Westland," Lyle said. "He might find the proper treatment."

"Is this all legal?" Sunny said.

"Absolutely," Lyle said. "Right papers, right judge, we can get him committed to the Rackley Young Adult Center."

"In Westland?"

"Yes," Lyle said. "It's a secure facility."

"My God," Sunny said. "I don't know. I need to talk with Elwood."

"Of course," Lyle said. "Is there somewhere I can reach you?"

Sunny stood and smiled.

"I'll call you," she said.

She put out her hand. He took it in his right and covered it with his left and shook it warmly.

"I can help you," he said.

"I think you can," Sunny said. "I just have to talk with Elwood."

Lyle held her hand for another moment, then released it as if he didn't want to, and Sunny left the office and took the elevator down to the parking garage.

34

JESSE GATHERED THEM in the squad room: Suit, Molly, Peter Perkins.

"We got a couple murders in town," Jesse said. "Let's talk about them."

"Moynihan and Reggie Galen knew each other in jail," Peter said.

Jesse nodded.

"They pretty much ran their wing of Garrison," Peter said. "They were tough guys, and they started out watching each other's back."

"What was their connection?" Jesse said.

"They were white," Perkins said.

"And the trouble was racial," Jesse said.

"Yes," Perkins said.

"Often is," Jesse said.

"People at Garrison told me that they were both pretty scary. And they both had a rep, and they both had outside connections. Word got around. After a while, they were in charge."

"Leadership qualities," Molly said.

Jesse smiled.

"Know who the outside connections were?" Jesse said.

"Nope."

"They got out at the same time?" Jesse said.

" 'Bout a month apart," Perkins said.

Jesse nodded.

"Anything else?" he said.

"All I could find out at Garrison," Perkins said.

Jesse walked to the end of the squad room and looked out the window at the Public Works parking lot.

"Okay," he said, looking out the window. "One of the outside contacts who belonged initially to Knocko was a big construction guy on the South Shore named Neal Bangston. His twin daughters married Knocko and Reggie."

"Jesus," Perkins said. "So, what's it mean?"

Jesse turned.

"No idea," Jesse said. "Suit?"

"The two daughters, Roberta and Rebecca, are identical twins," Suit said. "And they promote it. Dress alike, same hairstyle, same hair color, same makeup." He looked at Molly. "I think. Go everyplace together. Drive the same kind of car. You can't tell 'em apart."

"Usually," Perkins said, "twins are, like, the other way. You know, dress different and stuff."

"Well, these twins don't," Suit said. "And when they were in high school we found out that they used to have sex with each other's boyfriends and stuff like that."

"Known in high school as the Bang Bang Twins," Jesse said.

"Known and loved," Perkins said.

"Oh, don't be so piggy," Molly said.

Perkins grinned.

"So we figured it would be a good idea to see if they were still doing that kind of thing," Suit said.

"Because?" Molly said.

"Because we didn't know," Suit said.

"Where have I heard that before," Molly said.

Suit ignored her.

"They both went to Paulus College," he said. "Roomed together, of course. So I went over there, talked with people, got hold of some alumni from their class . . . and, yeah, they were still Bang Banging in college."

Suit went to the coffeemaker and poured some coffee. He offered the cup toward Molly; she shook her head. So he kept it and walked back to the conference table.

"What about me," Perkins said.

"Get your own," Suit said. "We lost track of them for a time, and then they surfaced, marrying Knocko and Reggie about four months apart."

"And they were connected to the twins' father," Molly said.

"Yeah," Suit said. "Jesse can tell you about that."

"Got a lot of this from a state police detective in the Norfolk DA's office," Jesse said. "With a little help from Rita Fiore."

"She's such a little helper," Molly said.

Jesse outlined what Traxal had told him.

"Ah," Molly said. "That's why you're so interested in the twins' sex life."

"If they were still Bang Bang," Jesse said, "it might have something to do with the murders."

"Yes," Molly said, and looked at Suit.

"Know anything about that?" she said.

Suit smiled and nodded.

"In fact, I do," he said.

STARTED," Suit said, "the way you would. Check out their social circle, talk to their friends, see if there was somebody knew something."

Suit shook his head.

"No social circle?" Molly said.

"None that I could find," Suit said. "Everybody who knew the ladies said they were nice. But nobody knew them very well."

"So, what did you do?" Molly said.

Molly's something, Jesse thought. *Suit's proud of himself, and she's helping him tell about it.*

"I went back door," Suit said. "I got a license picture from the registry and took it around to the motels in the area."

"Which one?" Perkins said.

Suit looked slightly annoyed. It was his moment, and he didn't like the interruption.

"Which one what?" Suit said.

"Which one you get a picture of?"

"What's the difference," Suit said. "They look exactly the same."

"Just wondering," Perkins said.

"It took a while," Suit said. "But I was guessing they weren't playing their game at home."

"They might have been," Perkins said.

Suit took a breath.

"Sure," he said. "But if they were, it gave me no place to look and nothing to do."

Perkins nodded. Jesse remembered saying that to Suit on the first case they ever worked. If there's two possibilities, take the one that gives you someplace to go. *Kid's a learner,* Jesse thought.

"So, I found a clerk at the Beach House in Danvers . . . which ain't on the beach and ain't a house. . . . This clerk remembered her checking in couple of times."

"Which one?" Perkins said.

"See my answer above," Suit said. "He remembers how good-looking she was, and very nice, checking in with a small suitcase in the middle of the day."

"She use her own name?" Jesse said.

"Bangston," Suit said. "Rebecca Bangston."

"So it was Rebecca," Perkins said. "Not Roberta."

"Who knows," Suit said. "We ran back through the registrations and found a bunch of Bangstons. Sometimes Rebecca, sometimes Roberta."

"You get the credit-card numbers?" Jesse said.

"Yep," Suit said. "Ran 'em past the credit-card company and got a pretty good list of motels and hotels where one or the other was used."

"What address does the credit-card company have for them?" Jesse said.

"Hempstead, Mass.," Suit said.

"Their mother?" Jesse said.

"Yep."

"Sounds like the Bang Bang Twins are alive and well," Jesse said.

"Now what?" Molly said.

"We'll look at the list," Jesse said.

THEY HAD COME in Spike's Lincoln Navigator. Spike was too big for Sunny's car. The Navigator was parked behind them, on a side road west of Framingham. They were standing in some woods, looking at the Rackley Young Adult Center, which appeared, from the front, like an expensive prep school, with a broad, welcoming walkway leading across a pleasant lawn to the front door. A chain-link fence enclosed the back lawn and ran up to the corners of the building. From the back it looked more like a prison.

"Here we go," Sunny said, and punched a number on her cell phone.

"This is Jessica Stone," she said. "With the State Inspectional Services. May I speak with the director. Yes, Dr. Patton."

Spike nodded.

"Done your homework," he murmured.

Sunny put her hand over the phone and nodded.

"Dr. Patton?" she said, when he came on the phone. "Jessica Stone, State Inspectional Services. We have reason to believe that you are harboring a fugitive."

"Fugitive?" Patton said.

"Cheryl DeMarco," Sunny said.

"We have no one here by that name," Patton said.

"Perhaps she's under another name," Sunny said. "In any case, I did not call you to debate. We will be at your office at nine a.m. with a bench warrant. If you do not produce her, we will search the facility."

"You can't be serious," Patton said.

"Don't produce her tomorrow," Sunny said. "You'll see how serious I am."

She turned off the cell phone.

"State Inspectional Services?" Spike said. "Do you even know what that is?"

"No," Sunny said. "But I'll bet he doesn't, either."

"And excuse me, but exactly how does a bench warrant differ from a regular warrant."

"No idea," Sunny said. "Heard it once on *Law and Order*."

"And you figure they'll panic and try to get her out of there before you descend on them in the morning."

"My guess," Sunny said.

"And we'll be here to take her away from them."

"Yes," Sunny said. "I checked out the entire building yesterday. If they want to get her out, they have to come out the front door and walk down the long path to the street. The rest is fenced, with no gate."

"What if Patton doesn't fall for it?" Spike said.

"What have we lost?" Sunny said. "We've poked a stick into the hive. Something will happen."

"Unless the kid isn't there," Spike said.

"Unless that," Sunny said.

"This a legitimate place?" Spike said.

"I would guess partially, but they cut some corners," Sunny said.

"How about the good doctor?"

"Dr. Abraham Patton," Sunny said. "He has an Ed.D. in educational statistics."

"What's that got to do with running a treatment center?"

"Not much," Sunny said. "But it entitles him to call himself Doctor."

"Of course, credentials aren't everything," Spike said. "I had shrinks with all the right degrees, didn't help me at all."

"You were seeing shrinks?" Sunny said.

"When I was worried about if I was gay," Spike said.

"You are gay," Sunny said.

"Gayer than laughter," Spike said. "But I couldn't quite figure out how I could be a tough guy. . . ."

"Which you certainly are," Sunny said.

"Got the build for it," Spike said. "But I had to figure out that being gay didn't mean I wasn't tough."

"Somebody helped you with that," Sunny said.

"One of the shrinks was good."

"You're not so bad yourself," Sunny said.

"That's true," Spike said. "I did the work. But I did the work with the others and nothing came of it. . . . They were trying to cure me."

"Think how different we'd be," Sunny said, "if you weren't gay."

"Your loss," Spike said.

"I don't know," Sunny said. "You're awful big."

"Anyway," Spike said. "Even if he is very good, and even if they're legit, he's not going to want a lot of attention paid."

"Because his credentials raise questions?"

"They do," Spike said. "And it wouldn't help business if they came under public discussion."

"Wow," Sunny said. " 'Under public discussion.' Don't you talk good."

"A natural poet," Spike said.

"If my girlish calculations are correct," Sunny said, "it's considerably shorter from these trees to the road than it is from the front door to the road."

"So," Spike said. "We stay here, and when they appear we dash out before they get her into the car."

"And you dazzle them with your rhetoric," Sunny said.

"Or something," Spike said.

"You have a gun," Sunny said.

"Yep."

"Think you'll need it?"

"Usually don't," Spike said.

37

IT WAS QUIET in the woods. There was a breeze, which kept the bugs from bothering them.

"What did that shrink say that worked for you?" Sunny said.

"Said I couldn't repress a part of myself and expect all the other parts to work well."

"Was he a gay shrink?"

"No."

"How do you know," Sunny said.

"I asked him," Spike said.

Sunny smiled.

"That would be you," she said.

"How you doing with Silverman?" Spike said.

"Dr. Silverman," Sunny said. "I can't think of her as Silverman."

"How you and she doing?"

"I feel I'm getting someplace."

"You know where yet?"

"No."

"You'll know," Spike said.

"I hope so," Sunny said.

"She gay?" Spike said.

"That's not germane to our therapy," Sunny said.

"Jesus," Spike said. "You got the shrink talk down. You think she might be gay?"

"If she is," Sunny said, "she's the lipstickiest lesbian I've ever seen."

A little after eight at night, a small gray Honda SUV pulled up in front of the center and parked on the road.

"Here she comes," Sunny said.

"You were right," Spike said.

After a moment, Cheryl DeMarco came out the front door with two orderlies in white coats. Each held an arm. She seemed passive. Behind them came a tallish man in a business suit with a stethoscope around his neck. When they were near the Honda, Sunny came out of the trees and stood between them and the car. Spike stood beside her.

"What's this?" the tallish man said.

"We're taking Cheryl," Sunny said.

Cheryl showed little interest.

"You can't do that," the tallish man said.

"Spike," Sunny said.

Spike shuffled his feet into some sort of fighting stance and hit one of the orderlies with a straight left to the nose. The orderly let go of Cheryl's arm and put his hands up to his face. He was bleeding. In rhythm Spike hit the other orderly with a right cross. The orderly fell down. Sunny took Cheryl's arm and led her toward Spike's car. The orderly with the bloody nose took a black leather sap from his hip pocket and tried to hit Spike with it. Spike stepped inside the looping swing and blocked it with both forearms, then hit the orderly on the side of the head with a backswing. The orderly dropped the blackjack as he went down. Spike kicked it away. Spike looked at the tallish man. The tallish man backed away. Both orderlies were now on the ground.

"See," Spike said. "We can do that."

Spike looked at the tallish man for another moment. On the road behind him the Honda drove away. Spike ignored it. He looked up the road to where Sunny and Cheryl were getting into his car. Then he looked back at the tallish man.

"Dr. Patton, I presume," Spike said.

"Yes," Patton said. "I'm in charge here."

"No," Spike said. "You ain't."

He reached out and yanked the stethoscope from Patton's neck.

"Don't hurt me," Patton said.

"Fucking fraud," Spike said.

He tossed the stethoscope onto the roadway. Then he turned and went toward his SUV, walking sedately. No one attempted to stop him.

When he got there, Sunny was in the backseat with Cheryl.

Cheryl was quiet, looking at nothing. Spike got in and started the car.

"She's sedated," Sunny said.

Spike looked in the rearview mirror. No one was following.

"Where you want to go?" Spike said.

"My place," Sunny said.

Spike headed up the side road toward Route 9.

"Why not Paradise," Spike said. "You got some clout with the cops there. Case there's trouble."

"I'm Phil Randall's daughter," Sunny said.

"Ah, yes," Spike said. "I guess you got some clout in Boston."

"Detective," Cheryl said.

"Yes," Sunny said. "Sunny Randall. We talked at the Renewal House."

"Mother," Cheryl said.

"You want your mother?"

Cheryl shook her head.

"Okay," Sunny said. "We'll go to my place and you can stay with me until the dope wears off and we can decide what to do."

Cheryl looked at Spike.

"Him?" Cheryl said.

"Spike," Sunny said.

"I'll stay with you, too," Spike said.

38

JESSE SAT with Suit and Molly in his office.

"Who's on the desk?" Jesse said.

"Eddie Cox," Molly said.

Jesse nodded.

"We have a married woman who fools around, and then one day her husband turns up dead," he said. "Normally, you'd figure it was the wife."

"But . . ." Molly said.

"But the woman has a history of swapping with her sister," Jesse said.

"So you'd think they'd swap husbands," Suit said.

"But if they were swapping husbands," Jesse said, "then why the motels? Why not walk next door?"

"Maybe the husbands weren't enough," Suit said.

"Nobody would swap with Knocko Moynihan," Molly said. Both men stared at her.

"He's a pig," Molly said.

"He was a pig when Roberta married him," Jesse said.

"Maybe not," Molly said.

"But you'd swap with Reggie?" Suit said.

"I wouldn't swap with anybody," Molly said. "But Reggie's not a pig like Knocko was."

"These are very odd women," Jesse said.

"You bet," Molly said. "But a three-way with Knocko? I don't know why Roberta married him. But Rebecca didn't marry him, and I'm betting she wouldn't have sex with him at gunpoint."

"Woman's intuition," Suit said.

"You bet," Molly said. "Why we make better cops."

Jesse got up and walked around the office. He picked up his baseball glove from the top of a cabinet and rubbed his fist in the pocket.

"Rawlings," he said.

"What?" Molly said.

"It's a Rawlings glove," Jesse said.

"You used it when you played," Molly said.

"Yep."

They were all silent for a time as Jesse stood with his glove. Then he took it off, and put it back on top of the cabinet, and went back and sat down behind his desk.

"We got another victim, too," he said.

"Ognowski," Suit said.

Jesse nodded.

"You think the Bang Bang Twins . . . were, ah, doing business with Ognowski?"

"Let's check with Ms. Intuition," Jesse said.

Molly was quiet for a moment.

Then she said, "Maybe."

"That's all?" Suit said. "'Maybe'?"

"It would make more sense if they were both practicing their craft with Reggie," Molly said.

"Why?"

"It just would," she said. "It seems somehow more incestuous."

"Incestuous?" Suit said.

"Twins sharing the same lovers?" Molly said. "There has to be something incestuous going on."

"Christ," Suit said. "Jesse?"

"Don't know much about it," Jesse said. "But I know someone who does."

39

Y OU WANT ME to explain repressed incest, once removed,"
Dix said. "Among people I've never met?"

"Yuh," Jesse said.

"While I'm at it, would you like me to help you with your
mental health?"

"Sure," Jesse said.

Dix sat back in his chair and put his feet up.

"Okay, tell me what you know," Dix said.

While Jesse told him, Dix looked steadily at Jesse and never
moved. When Jesse was through, Dix remained motionless and
silent for what seemed to Jesse a full minute.

Then he said, "First, I'm sure you understand that this is not
psychotherapy."

Jesse nodded.

"I am at best an educated consultant in this."

"Puts you ahead of me," Jesse said.

"You've been a cop long enough to know the difference between what you speculate about a suspect you haven't met and what you learn in an interview."

"Tell me what you speculate," Jesse said.

"Let's see what we've got here," Dix said. "They are identical twins."

"Yes," Jesse said.

"They were raised together simultaneously in the same environment."

"Yes."

"The father was a successful philanderer and an associate, at least, of criminals."

"Yes."

"The mother is rigid and religious."

"Yes."

"The twins are not close to their mother."

"Doesn't seem so," Jesse said.

"But they are close to each other," Dix said. "They dress alike, act alike. Apparently think alike."

"I have the sense that the parents encouraged them in that," Jesse said. "Mother thought it was God's will. Father thought it was cute."

"In some cases when two people are having sex with the same third party, one can speculate that they are trying in fact to access each other," Dix said.

"Through an intermediary," Jesse said.

"Yes."

"You think that's what's going on here."

"Not exactly," Dix said. "They might both be trying to access the father through a surrogate."

"And married the surrogates that seemed most like Dad?" Jesse said.

"Maybe," Dix said.

"Why together?" Jesse said.

"They are almost each other," Dix said. "They may experience life as each other. It may alleviate guilt to be with each other. Perhaps it also cements their each-otherness."

"What about Ognowski?"

"Maybe Molly's right," Dix said. "Maybe Knocko was too repellent for one . . . or, for that matter, for both. In any case, it doesn't change anything. The pathology seems firmly established, and if the usual way didn't work, it would find another."

"But we don't know if any of this is true," Jesse said.

"No," Dix said. "It's an educated hypothesis which explains the data we have."

"It's a guess," Jesse said.

"Exactly," Dix said.

"And even if it's accurate," Jesse said, "what good does it do me?"

"Not my department," Dix said.

"Better to know than not to know, I suppose."

"Of course, we don't actually know anything," Dix said.

"It's an educated hypothesis which explains the data we have," Jesse said.

"Well said."

"But it still doesn't explain two murders," Jesse said.

"No," Dix said. "It doesn't. But it might help define the area of speculation."

"Man," Jesse said. "Sometimes you talk just like a shrink."

"There's probably a reason for that," Dix said.

"Where do I go from here?" Jesse said.

"I don't know," Dix said.

"You're supposed to know."

Dix smiled.

"I never promised you a rose garden," he said.

"No one seems to," Jesse said.

They were silent for a moment.

Then Dix said, "We have some time left."

Jesse nodded.

"Why was I so taken with them?" he said.

"The twins," Dix said.

"Yeah. I was so envious of them that I went on a bender," Jesse said.

"And why was it you were so envious?" Dix said.

Jesse said, "Why wouldn't I be?"

Dix moved his shoulders in something that might have been a shrug.

"Everybody wants to be loved," Jesse said.

"Love manifests," Dix said, "in many ways."

"Wow," Jesse said. "That's a real shrink phrase."

"Feeling some anger?" Dix said. "At me?"

Jesse shrugged.

"Why do you suppose you're angry?" Dix said.

Jesse took in a deep breath and let it out in slow exasperation.

"Because you're leading me to face something I don't want to face," he said.

Dix said nothing.

"They were both so submissive," Jesse said. "So . . ." He made a circular motion with his hand as he searched for the word.

"Self-abnegating?" Dix said.

"Hoo-ha!" Jesse said. "Self-abnegating."

"You know what it means," Dix said.

Jesse nodded.

"And you're right," he said. "I loved how self-abnegating they were."

"So, if they put themselves aside . . . ?" Dix said.

"Then they totally belonged to the husband," Jesse said.

Dix waited. He leaned back a little farther. His elbows were on the arms of his chair. His hands were folded in front of him. He rubbed the balls of his thumbs lightly together.

"What woman would want that?" Jesse said.

Dix waited.

"What man would want a woman to be like that?" Jesse said.

Dix waited.

"I don't like women like that," Jesse said.

Dix moved his head slightly. It might have been a nod.

"A woman like that couldn't leave me," Jesse said.

Dix nodded.

"Jesus," Jesse said. "I was asking Jenn to do things she couldn't do, and shouldn't."

"Probably," Dix said.

"And then I blamed her when she cheated."

"Tough place for Jenn to be," Dix said.

"Why the hell am I like that?" Jesse said.

Dix looked at his watch.

"Don't know," he said. "Maybe we'll find out. Maybe we'll never know. But perhaps you won't make the same mistake again."

Jesse nodded. When he left the office, he felt a little dizzy. And his head felt overused.

40

W HAT'S THAT EASEL?" Cheryl said.
They were sitting at Sunny's kitchen counter. Sunny had
toasted some English muffins for breakfast, and they were eat-
ing the muffins and drinking coffee.

"I'm painting a picture," Sunny said.

"You're a painter?"

"Sort of," Sunny said.

Cheryl went down and looked at the painting.

"It's a dog," Cheryl said.

"Yes."

"Is it your dog?"

"It was," Sunny said. "Her name was Rosie."

"She dead?"

"Yes."

Cheryl walked back to the counter.

"That's too bad," she said. "I never had a dog."

Sunny nodded.

"Tell me how you ended up in the Rackley center," she said.

"I was walking back toward the Renewal House," Cheryl said. "And a car stopped ahead of me and a lady got out of the backseat and said could I help her with directions. So I say sure, and the lady yells into the car, 'Show her the map,' or something like that. I lean in to look at the map and the lady pushes me in and the guy grabs me and the lady gets in behind me and shuts the door and the car drove away."

"They say anything?" Sunny asked.

"Lady told me to shut up or I'd get hurt. I was scared. I did what they said. And they brought me to the school or whatever it was, and the white coats came and took me in and gave me some kind of shot in my arm and locked me in my room."

"Anyone ever talk with you?"

"Dr. Patton," she said.

"What did he tell you," Sunny said.

"He told me that the center was here to help, and I was there because my parents were worried about me."

"Did your parents come to see you?"

"I don't think so," Cheryl said. "I was kind of woozy most of the time."

"I've got a doctor appointment for you later today."

"How come I need a doctor?" Cheryl said.

"I don't think there's anything wrong with you," Sunny said. "It just seems like the right thing to do."

"Okay," Cheryl said. "Will you go with me?"

"Of course."

"What about that guy?"

"Spike?"

"The big, fat one," Cheryl said.

"Spike's built like a bear," Sunny said. "He's not as fat as he looks."

"Is he your boyfriend?" Cheryl said.

"No."

"Does he, like, work for you?"

"No, Spike is my best friend," Sunny said.

"But not your boyfriend."

"No," Sunny said. "Spike is gay."

"Wow," Cheryl said. "He doesn't look gay."

"I guess he feels gay," Sunny said.

"I thought gay guys were all, you know, fa-la-la," Cheryl said.

"Spike is not fa-la-la," Sunny said.

"Didn't he hammer the two white coats?"

"He did," Sunny said.

"I guess he's not," Cheryl said.

"So get showered and changed," Sunny said. "And I'll take you over to MGH to see my gyno."

"I don't think I like gynos much," Cheryl said.

"You've been to a gyno already?"

"Yes. My mother kept worrying I'd get pregnant. I didn't like him."

"You'll like Beth Thomson," Sunny said. "She's fun."

"The gyno my mother took me to was a man," Cheryl said.

"After that we'll go see your parents," Sunny said.

"No."

"Yeah, we gotta do that," Sunny said. "I'll be with you. We'll visit and leave. But we need to confront them."

"Why?"

"We need—you need, and I need—to figure out why they had you kidnapped."

"They don't want me to be with the Renewal."

Sunny nodded.

"We probably need to know a little more about why," Sunny said. "We also need to figure out how you and they can have a relationship."

"I don't want one," Cheryl said. "And neither do they."

"So, you're ready to be on your own at eighteen?" Sunny said.

"Todd will take care of me."

"And who takes care of Todd? What does either of you do for a living?"

"We'll make it work," Cheryl said. "We love each other."

"Might be able to make out better if your parents contributed to your support until you sort of got your feet under you."

"They won't do that," Cheryl said.

"Maybe we can insist," Sunny said.

" 'Insist'?"

"We sort of have the goods on them," Sunny said.

Cheryl stared at her.

"Can Spike come?" Cheryl said, after a moment of staring.

Sunny smiled.

"Sure," she said.

"I'd like to see my father yell at Spike," Cheryl said.

"He might yell," Sunny said. "I think Spike will remain calm."

"I bet my father would be scared of Spike."

"If your father has a brain," Sunny said.

"I'll go if Spike comes," Cheryl said.

"He'll come," Sunny said.

41

THE NIGHT WAS fading outside Jesse's office window when Healy came in. He walked to a file cabinet, took a glass off the top, walked back around Jesse's desk, took a seat, and held the glass out. Jesse smiled and took a bottle out of his desk drawer and poured Healy an inch or so of scotch.

"You gonna join me?" Healy said.

Jesse paused for a moment.

"*I don't think you're an alcoholic,*" Sunny had said. *See if she's right.*

He got another glass and poured himself a drink. He made a "here's to you" gesture at Healy and took in a small swallow. Healy drank.

"What's new with your homicides," Healy said.

Jesse leaned back in his chair and put his feet up on the desktop.

"Lemme tell you about the Bang Bang Twins," he said.

Healy sipped his scotch.

"Okay," he said.

Jesse told him.

"Guess we misjudged them a little," Healy said.

Jesse shrugged and drank some scotch.

"You think the four of them were playing house?" Healy said.

"The Moynihans and the Galens?" Jesse said.

"Yeah."

"Molly says that no woman would play house with Knocko," Jesse said.

"I hope she's right," Healy said.

"Yeah, it's not an appealing thought," Jesse said.

"You think they were both fucking Ognowski?" Healy said.

"Maybe," Jesse said.

"If they were, now they aren't," Healy said.

Jesse nodded.

"You know what I'm thinking about?" Jesse said.

"I'd worry about myself," Healy said, "if I did."

"I'm thinking that this Bang Bang thing is a long-standing pathology. . . ."

"You been talking to your shrink," Healy said.

"I have," Jesse said. "But that aside, it seems like these women need to do what they do, and if they don't have Knocko, or Ognowski, what do they do?"

"Reggie?" Healy said.

166

"Maybe," Jesse said.

"On the other hand," Healy said, "if Reggie's part of the game, they had him before."

Jesse nodded.

"Two guys were killed," he said. "If it's the Bang Bang game. Which any way you turn it suggests they wanted more than Reggie."

"Does," Healy said.

His glass was empty. He held it out and Jesse filled it.

"Be good to know what they are doing now," Jesse said.

"Surveillance?"

"Round the clock?" Jesse said. "Out on Paradise Neck? I got a twelve-person department."

"Twelve's enough," Healy said.

"Town life goes on," Jesse said. "Parking laws gotta be enforced. Drunks gotta be hauled in for the night. Domestic disturbances have to be dealt with. Rabid raccoons have to be shot."

"Yeah, yeah," Healy said. "I get it."

"You want to loan me some people?" Jesse said.

"No."

"Figured you wouldn't."

"Can't," Healy said.

"No," Jesse said. "I know you can't. You got your own rabid raccoons to shoot."

"Surveillance camera wouldn't solve your problem," Healy said.

"No."

"You need more people."

"I do," Jesse said.

"But even if you had more people," Healy said, "and you're able to spot them in delicato, so to speak, what have you got."

"Maybe some leverage," Jesse said. "Right now they're just the grieving family."

"Maybe you can establish some connection to Ognowski's killing," Healy said. "That'd give you some leverage."

"Speaking of grieving family," Jesse said.

"Ognowski's got family?"

"His old man is around. He's about the size of Malden," Jesse said. "And he's gonna find out who killed his son."

"Maybe you should let him," Healy said.

"Let him? I can't even find him," Jesse said.

"I'll look in the files," Healy said.

He finished his second drink and stood.

"Keep me posted," Healy said.

"Sure," Jesse said.

When Healy was gone, Jesse washed Healy's glass in the sink. He looked at his own empty glass. He'd had only one drink. He could have one more. He poured some and put the bottle away, and sat and sipped the scotch and thought about how to get past the blank wall he kept bumping into in the two murders. When he was done with his second drink he sat for a time looking at the empty glass, and thinking about the murders, and about a third drink, and about Sunny Randall.

"I like that woman," Jesse said aloud to his empty glass.

He sat for a time longer. Then he got up and left the office and went home.

SPIKE WAS DRIVING. Sunny sat beside him. Cheryl was in the backseat. Sunny was on her cell phone.

"Mrs. Markham? This is Sunny Randall. . . . Cheryl is with me, and we're coming to visit you. I think your husband should be there, too. . . . That is not my problem. He needs to be there."

She ended the call, turned the cell phone off, and turned sideways in her seat so she could see Cheryl.

"Golf," Sunny said.

"He plays golf every Saturday morning with people from work."

"How exciting for him," Spike said.

"I think it's icky and boring," Cheryl said.

"Ever play?" Sunny said.

"No."

"Hard to be so sure," Sunny said.

"What if we go there and they grab me?" Cheryl said.

"We grab you back," Sunny said.

"You and Spike," Cheryl said.

"Yep."

"What if they call the cops?" Cheryl said.

"They won't," Sunny said.

"How can you be sure?"

"Do you think your parents want to be publicly involved in a case where they arranged the kidnapping of their own daughter?"

Cheryl thought about it.

"That would be bad for him at work, wouldn't it," Cheryl said.

"Not so good for either of them," Sunny said. "At the country club, either."

"And you'd really tell?" Cheryl said.

"I'd do what I thought was in your best interest," Sunny said. "But the threat that I might make will prevent the police from getting involved."

Cheryl nodded.

"They care a ton about what people think," she said.

"Everybody cares some," Sunny said.

"Except me," Spike said.

"Sure," Sunny said. "How about those two young guys you talk to all the time when they come to the restaurant?"

"That's different," Spike said. "They're really cute."

"The trick is," Sunny said to Cheryl, "not to let it make you do things that are bad for you."

"You care what people think?" Cheryl said.

"Yes," Sunny said.

"You ever do things that are bad for you?"

"Yes," Sunny said.

She smiled at Cheryl.

"Being an adult," Sunny said, "allows me to instruct you in things I can't do, either."

"You don't talk much like an adult," Cheryl said.

"I'll get better as I get older," Sunny said.

Spike pulled the Navigator up in front of the Markham house.

Sunny looked at Cheryl.

"Here we go," Sunny said.

Elsa Markham opened the front door.

"Cheryl," Elsa said. "What on earth are you doing with these people?"

Cheryl shrugged.

Behind his wife, John Markham looked past his daughter at Spike.

"Who is this?" Markham said to Sunny.

"My walker," Sunny said.

"How y'all doin'?" Spike said, and smiled widely.

"Are you planning on coming home?" Elsa said. "Is that what this is all about?"

"May we come in?" Sunny said.

"We can talk here," Markham said.

"No," Sunny said. "We can't. We're not selling vacuum cleaners. We need to come in and sit and talk like civilized adults."

"About what?" Elsa said.

"Your daughter's well-being, kidnapping, stuff like that," Sunny said.

"What on earth are you talking about?" Elsa said.

"Oh, for crissake," Markham said. "Let them in, Elsa."

She hesitated.

"Goddamn it, Elsa," Markham said.

Elsa almost jumped back, and Sunny led Cheryl and Spike into the house. They sat in the living room, where Sunny had sat before.

"Now," Markham said. "What's all this about?"

"Just so we don't waste time," Sunny said, "I've spoken with Don Cahill and Harry Lyle. And I've been to the Rackley center, and Spike and I have spoken, somewhat briefly, with Abraham Patton, Ed.D."

Elsa said, "I simply don't know what you're talking about."

Markham said, "Elsa, be quiet. Not another word. I'm calling a lawyer."

"Egad," Spike said. "A lawyer!"

"I'm not the police, Mr. Markham," Sunny said. "You don't need a lawyer."

Markham picked a cell phone up from the top of the coffee table.

"You won't need to talk unless you wish to," Sunny said. "All you need to do is listen to what I say."

Markham held the cell phone, but he didn't dial.

"You arranged to kidnap your daughter and, as you can

probably tell, I can prove it," Sunny said. "The chain of connection is apparent. Too many people are involved. And none of them are likely to go under protecting you."

Markham was silent. Sunny held his stare.

"What has she been telling you?" Elsa said.

No one paid her any attention.

"You'd testify against your own parents?" Markham said to Cheryl.

Cheryl nodded.

"She'd testify," Sunny said, "as to what happened to her. As I would testify about what I know. The court, and of course the media, would respond as it saw fit."

"What if I asked you to leave?"

"We'd go."

"What if I asked you to leave Cheryl with us."

"She's free to stay if she wishes," Sunny said.

Cheryl said, "No."

"Which apparently she does not," Sunny said.

"And if I tried to prevent her from leaving, would he intercede?" Markham said.

"Oh, sure," Spike said.

Markham nodded. He put down the cell phone.

"What do you want?" he said.

Sunny could see why Markham had advanced in business. He was sort of all self-centered pomposity when you met him, but when it all hit the fan, he became quite controlled.

"I want you to let your daughter lead her life," Sunny said. "I want you to treat her as if you were loving parents. And I want you to support her as you would were she living at home."

"You think we are not loving parents?" Elsa said.

"I'm convinced that you're not," Sunny said. "But that's not the argument."

Without looking at his wife, Markham said, "Shut up, Elsa."

To Sunny he said, "Agreed. How much?"

"We'll work out the amounts and the means of conveyance," Sunny said. "And to be clear, if everything doesn't go the way we agree, I'll blow my whistle to the cops and the press."

"E-mail me the amount," Markham said, handing her a card.

"She may or may not stay in touch with you; that's up to her," Sunny said. "But I will stay in touch with her, and if you are interested, I'll keep you informed."

"Yes," Elsa said.

"She had a physical this morning at Mass General, and except for some traces of tranquilizer still lingering in her system, she's healthy. Couple more days and the tranq will have dissipated and she'll be fine."

Elsa nodded.

Sunny said, "Anything you want to say, Cheryl?"

"No," Cheryl said.

"All we tried to do for you," Elsa said to her daughter.

"That's aimless," Sunny said, and stood.

Cheryl stood. Spike had never sat.

"We can find the door," Sunny said.

Neither Elsa nor Markham said a word, nor did they move. Sunny and Cheryl and Spike found the door. And went out.

44

ALKED TO Mike Mayo in Hempstead," Suit said to Jesse.
"Mother saves the credit-card bills for one of the girls to
pick up."

"She hasn't got any?" Jesse said.

"She has. She gave them to Mayo. There's no charges on
them."

"None?"

"Nope."

"Must have used that card only for sex," Jesse said.

Suit nodded.

Molly called Jesse on the intercom.

"Mr. Ognowski is here waiting to see you."

Jesse waved Suit out of the room.

"Waiting?"

"Yes, sir."

"Send him in," Jesse said. "Try not to get trampled."

In a moment Nicolas Ognowski rumbled into Jesse's office and sat down.

"More patient today," Jesse said.

"I can be patient," Ognowski said.

Jesse nodded.

"I ask around about you," Ognowski said.

Jesse nodded.

"I see myself you are not afraid, you do not back down," Ognowski said. "Other people tell me you keep your word."

Jesse nodded again.

"They also say you good cop."

"I am," Jesse said.

"And you care, about being good cop."

"I do," Jesse said.

"And you sometimes drink too much," Ognowski said.

"I do," Jesse said.

"Reggie Galen is a criminal," Ognowski said. "The dead one, Knocko, him, too."

"I know," Jesse said.

"I know a lot about criminal," Ognowski said.

"I guessed that," Jesse said.

"My Petey work for Galen. So when he die, I ask around. I learn that Galen and Knocko in business together. I learn about a man named Bangston they in business with, and that they marry Bangston's daughters."

"Pretty good," Jesse said.

"People say Bangston daughters will fuck anybody."

"The Bang Bang Twins," Jesse said.

"What is Bang Bang?" Ognowski said.

"Slang for fucking," Jesse said.

Ognowski nodded.

"Somebody like Bang Bang," Ognowski said, "my Petey is ready."

"You think Petey was having sex with them?"

"Both?" Ognowski said. "I had not thought both. You think both?"

"Maybe," Jesse said. "That was their style. One or the other. You can't tell them apart, went to motels often."

"So she, they, Bang Bang their husband, no reason for motel."

"None," Jesse said.

"Bang Bang somebody else."

"Seems likely," Jesse said.

"You know all this I tell you?"

"Yes," Jesse said.

"And you do nothing?"

"Who killed Petey?" Jesse said.

Ognowski stared at Jesse for a moment. Then he nodded slowly.

"We do not know yet," Ognowski said.

"True," Jesse said.

"You have to know," Ognowski said.

"I do," Jesse said.

"But I do not. Maybe make them all . . ."

He put his fist out and opened it as if releasing a butterfly.

"Maybe none of them did it," Jesse said.

Ognowski shrugged.

"Maybe Knocko did it."

Ognowski shrugged again.

"Maybe Galen snuffed Knocko for killing Petey"

Ognowski sat silently for a moment, looking past Jesse at nothing.

Then he said, "I love my son. I get revenge, it won't bring him back, but I feel better."

Jesse nodded.

"He was my only son. When he learn what he need to learn working for other people, doing what he did, he will someday replace me."

"And now he won't," Jesse said.

"No," Ognowski said.

He paused and looked up at the ceiling, as if composing his next sentence.

Then he said, "Many places in this world, people know Nicolas Ognowski, and they do what he says because they fear him."

"And it's bad for business," Jesse said, "for anyone to kill Nicolas Ognowski's son and get away with it."

Ognowski nodded.

"That is the truth of it," he said.

"If anything happens to Galen or the two women," Jesse said, "I'll come looking for you."

"You will not find me," Ognowski said.

"How about they didn't do it and I catch the real killer later? How's that for business?"

"Could be better, but not so bad," Ognowski said. "At least there is blood for blood."

"Even if it's the wrong blood?" Jesse said.

"I can always return," Ognowski said.

"Next time would be harder," Jesse said.

"Might be," Ognowski said. "Does not mean it wouldn't happen."

"It might make more sense to give it a little time. Maybe between us we can come up with something."

"What?"

"No idea," Jesse said. "But the two of us ought to be able to come up with something."

Ognowski looked at Jesse for a time in silence.

"Give it a little while," Jesse said.

Ognowski kept looking at Jesse. Finally he stood and walked out of the office without saying anything else.

45

SHE HAD WATCHED him for two weeks, and almost every night he came here, to the Gray Gull, and sat at the bar. He drank bourbon on the rocks, and often left with a woman. Never the same woman. He was a big man and handsome. He had big muscles and, she noticed, he always wore short-sleeved shirts that displayed them. She sipped her vodka and tonic. It was a Friday night and the bar was crowded. But she had time. And she was patient. She waited, and finally when a seat opened at the bar next to him she went down the bar and took it. He glanced at her and then swung around on his bar stool to face her.

"I haven't seen you before," he said.

"I come sometimes," she said.

"By yourself?" he said.

"Yes."

"Can I buy you a drink?" he said.

"Yes," she said.

"Vodka tonic?" he said.

"Yes."

He gestured to one of the bartenders and ordered.

"You from around here?" he said.

"No."

"Where you from?"

"Brooklyn," she said.

"Brooklyn, huh?"

"Yes."

"Jesus," he said. "You don't talk much."

She smiled.

"Many men like that," she said.

He nodded.

"Okay," he said. "How come you're up here from Brooklyn?"

"My husband had work here."

"Husband?"

"Yes. No more."

"You're not married anymore?"

"No," she said.

The drinks came. He stirred the ice around in his drink with his forefinger before he picked it up.

"Looking for a new husband?" he said.

"No," she said.

"What are you looking for?" he said.

"I like men," she said.

He grinned and raised his glass to her.

"I'm one," he said.

"Yes," she said, and looked at him. "Big muscles."

He nodded.

"I try to stay in shape," he said.

"You work?"

"Sure," he said. "Whaddya think? I do private security for a guy lives on the Neck."

"You violent?" she said.

"Let's just say I don't look for trouble," he said. "But if someone else is looking for trouble, I'm happy to supply it."

She nodded.

"That excites me," she said.

"It does, huh?" he said. "Wanna go someplace, see what else we can think of that's exciting?"

"I have a place," she said.

"Excellent," he said.

"I will go into the ladies' room for a moment," she said. "Then we go to my place."

"You bet," he said. "What's your name?"

"Natalya," she said. "You?"

"Normie."

46

THE SECURITY at the gate of the late Knocko Moynihan was
just like the security at Reggie Galen's gate. But Jesse had
called in advance, and the guard waved him through.

Robbie Moynihan opened the door, wearing black slingback
heels and a short black linen sundress.

"Chief Stone," she said.

"Mrs. Moynihan," Jesse said.

"Oh, fah!" she said. "I've told you and told you, call me
Robbie."

"Sure," Jesse said.

He followed her toward the living room.

"Say it," Robbie said.

"Robbie," Jesse said.

"Very good," she said.

She gestured for him to sit in a chair.

"Sit," she said.

"Can you say Jesse?" he said.

She smiled.

"Sit, Jesse," she said. "Jesse, Jesse, Jesse!"

"Okay, Robbie, I guess we are pals."

"Absolutely," she said. "Would you like coffee? Or a drink?"

"Late for coffee," Jesse said. "Early for a drink."

"And you're on duty," Robbie said.

"Technically, I'm always on duty," Jesse said. "But in fact I'm here to see how you are."

"Not official business?" Robbie said.

"No."

"Well, then, you should be able to have a drink," she said. "I'm going to have some champagne, and I'll be offended if you don't at least have a little glass."

Jesse was silent for a moment.

Then he said, "Thank you, I'll have a glass."

"Good," she said. "Champagne is fun."

She went out and came back soon carrying two champagne flutes and an ice bucket with a bottle of Krug in it.

"I think opening champagne bottles is man's work," she said.

"I do, too," Jesse said.

Jesse opened the bottle, poured some into her glass and some into his. He raised his glass to her.

"Here's to better times," he said.

She smiled and raised her glass.

"Yes," she said. "You're very sweet to stop in. I admit I was feeling kind of blue."

"You have every reason," Jesse said.

He took a small sip. At least it was champagne. He found champagne easier to resist than other things.

"It's been hard," she said. "But my sister is here."

She drank the rest of her champagne and held her glass out. Jesse carefully filled it. Then she raised her glass to Jesse.

"Here's to you," she said. "And to catching the guy who did it."

She drank. Jesse took another restrained sip.

"It's slow going," he said.

"Do you have any leads?" she said.

"This and that," Jesse said. "Nothing very solid. We're assuming that the two murders are connected."

"Two? Oh, of course, poor Petey."

"You liked him?" Jesse said.

"Oh, yes. We both loved Petey."

"You and your sister."

She held out her glass, and Jesse filled it. The bottle was nearly empty. The flutes didn't hold very much, but she wasn't malingering.

"Yes," she said.

"You haven't heard from Ray Mulligan, have you?"

She leaned forward toward him with her forearms resting on her thighs, holding the flute in both hands.

"Jesse," she said. "Are you questioning me?"

"I don't mean to," Jesse said. "I guess I've been a cop too long."

She nodded and smiled. Her eyes were shiny.

"Plus, you are the chief of police," she said.

"That makes it worse," Jesse said.

"We believe in you, Jesse," she said. "We believe we can depend on you."

"Thank you," Jesse said.

They were quiet for a moment. Jesse could feel a subliminal sexual charge begin to seep into the room. He didn't know how he knew it. But he knew it. He'd felt it before, and he'd never been wrong. Jesse also noticed that she had not answered his question about Ray Mulligan.

She remained leaning forward, looking at him.

After a while, she said, "Do you like sex, Jesse?"

"Yes."

"Do the women you know like sex?"

"I think so," Jesse said.

She smiled.

"Do you approve of women who like sex?"

"Yes, I do," Jesse said.

The subliminal sexual charge was now nearly stifling. She picked up the champagne bottle and poured the little that remained into Jesse's glass, which was still more full than empty.

"Have you ever had sex with more than one woman, Jesse?" she said.

"Not at the same time," Jesse said.

She smiled and picked up the empty champagne bottle.

"I'll get us some more," she said.

She had drunk most of a bottle of champagne, but there was no slur to her speech, and her walk was perfectly steady as she went out of the room.

What happens when she comes back? Jesse thought.

THEY CAME IN TOGETHER, both wearing the little black sundress and the slingback heels. One of them carried a bottle of champagne. Even side by side, it was difficult to tell them apart.

"You ladies hang around the house together in the same outfit?" Jesse said.

"Actually," one of them said, "we do, sometimes. But when you called to say you were coming, we thought we might have some fun with you."

Jesse nodded.

"For instance, Robbie let you in. But I brought in the champagne."

"So you would be Becca," Jesse said.

"Yes," she said.

"How do you know?" Jesse said.

They both laughed.

"Would you like to see what's next?" Robbie said.

"Sure," Jesse said.

Robbie turned away from Becca. Becca unzipped the dress in the back. Then Robbie unzipped Becca, and they both turned toward Jesse and simultaneously slid the sundresses down and stepped out of them. Neither twin was wearing anything under the sundress.

"Heavenly days," Jesse said.

They both smiled. It was like watching a well-rehearsed dance team. They even stood alike. They radiated sweetness.

"Now," Robbie said, "we go in the bedroom. You undress and see if you can keep track of who's doing what to whom."

"Why would I want to?" Jesse said.

"It's part of the fun," Becca said.

Jesse sat and looked at them thoughtfully. They were gorgeous. And identical. They moved in a little circle, and Jesse lost track again of who was whom.

"The Bang Bang Twins," Jesse said.

They spoke in unison, "Don't say that."

"We don't like that name," one of them said.

How bizarre is this? Jesse thought. *I'm interrogating two naked women.*

"You play this game with Petey?" Jesse said.

It must be hard, he thought, *to stand around naked in front of someone fully clothed and be interrogated.*

"Jesse," one of them said. "You said this was a social call."

"Or Knocko?" Jesse said.

Again, they answered simultaneously.

"Don't be ridiculous," they said.

"What's wrong with Knocko?" Jesse said.

"He was a pig," one of them said.

The other one nodded vigorously.

"How about Reggie?" Jesse said. "He a pig, too?"

"No," they answered, and looked at each other and giggled.

"Stop thinking about that stuff," one of the sisters said. "Let's play."

"We could do it right here," the other sister said. "If you'd rather."

Jesse put his nearly full champagne glass on the coffee table and stood up.

"It's an exciting offer," he said. "But rule three in the chief-of-police manual says: no gang bangs."

The twins stared at him as he walked out.

I N THE G RAY G ULL, at their table for two, they could look
at the harbor and across at the Neck. It was early evening, and
the boats in the harbor moved gently at their moorings. The
light at that time of day had a faint blue tone. Sunny was drinking a glass of Riesling. Jesse sipped a beer.

"Both of them," Sunny said.

"Yep."

"Buck naked," Sunny said.

"Well," Jesse said. "They had shoes on."

"How was that?"

"New and different," Jesse said.

"Was it, ah, sexually stimulating?"

"Yes."

"But you didn't follow through," Sunny said.

"No."

"Why not?"

"It didn't seem like a good idea," Jesse said.

Sunny smiled.

"I haven't met many men," she said, "who think about how good an idea it is when confronted by a naked woman."

"I know," Jesse said. "I'm a little surprised, myself."

"Were you daunted by the fact there were two?"

"Maybe," Jesse said. "Never did anything but the standard one-on-one that I can recall."

"Maybe you were daunted by the fact that they might be murderers."

"That's daunting," Jesse said. "It's also daunting, if I ever got them into court, to explain to their defense attorney that yes, I did have sex with them both."

"The old cluster-fuck defense," Sunny said.

"That one," Jesse said.

"How did they take it?" Sunny said.

"The rejection?" Jesse said. "They just stared at me and didn't say a word."

"And you left," Sunny said.

"Yep."

"Probably hadn't heard 'no' before," Sunny said.

"A lot less than they've heard 'yes,' I'd guess," Jesse said.

"So, what'd you learn in this exercise?" Sunny said.

"You don't have to have sex with anyone who wants it?"

"Girls know that from puberty," Sunny said. "What'd you learn that might help you with the case. I assume that's why you got yourself into that situation."

"Clearly they were banging Petey," Jesse said. "Clearly they were not banging Knocko."

"Molly was right," Sunny said.

"Apparently," Jesse said. "And I would guess they're both banging Reggie."

"Infidelity and murder are not incompatible," Sunny said.

"Wow," Jesse said. "I wish I'd said that."

"Hell," Sunny said. "You wish you could."

They both laughed. The waitress brought them each another drink.

"Spike sent these over," she said.

"Tell him thank you," Jesse said.

"Want to hear about the menu?" the waitress said.

"Not yet. I'm right at a crucial point in the seduction," Jesse said.

"Oh," the waitress said. "You want some oysters."

"I'll let you know," Jesse said.

The waitress smiled and went away.

"One scenario," Jesse said. "His wife's bopping Petey. Knocko finds out. Kills Petey out of jealousy. Then finds out she's been bopping Reggie. Makes a run at Reggie and isn't good enough."

"What about Ray Mulligan?" Sunny said.

"Yeah," Jesse said. "That bothers me, too."

"It's sort of funny he gets rid of his boyhood friend and body-guard and gets murdered right after," Sunny said.

"It is," Jesse said. "Maybe the girls helped get rid of him."

"Why?"

"Maybe they wanted Knocko dead," Jesse said. "Maybe they liked Petey."

"So, who you think pulled the trigger?" Sunny said.

"Reggie?" Jesse said. "Or had Bob do it?"

"Revenge for Petey?" Sunny said.

"Maybe," Jesse said. "Maybe the Bang Bang Twins got him to do it."

"And what have you got to take to the DA?" Sunny said.

"Not much," Jesse said.

"'Not much' is a wild exaggeration," Sunny said. "You have nothing."

"Well," Jesse said. "Yes."

Sunny finished her first glass of wine and put it aside. She moved the glass that Spike had sent in front of her. Jesse was already on the second beer.

"Be nice if you could find Ray Mulligan," Sunny said.

"Yes," Jesse said. "If I can."

"You're the chief of police," Sunny said.

"Oh, right," Jesse said. "Of course I can find him."

The waitress returned.

"You ready to order?" she said.

Jesse looked at Sunny. Sunny nodded.

"Yes," Jesse said. "We can order."

"You want those oysters?" the waitress said.

"Bring him a dozen," Sunny said.

The waitress smiled and shot at Jesse with her forefinger.

I'VE BEEN THINKING," Sunny said.

Dr. Silverman nodded and cocked her head slightly, ready to listen.

"We talked a while ago about being incomplete," Sunny said.

"We talked of how you *felt* incomplete," Dr. Silverman said.

Sunny nodded.

"Anyway," she said, "I was thinking of my mother and sister."

Dr. Silverman gave a small encouraging nod.

"Your sister is older?" she said.

"Yes, and she's a mess, like my mother," Sunny said. "You know what they're like, I've told you about them."

"Might be useful to talk about them again."

"You've forgotten?" Sunny said.

"I do forget things," Dr. Silverman said. "But in this instance it's more of a therapeutic tool. If you reexamine the same thing in a different context, new things sometimes appear."

"My mother knows very little, and fears many things. But she pretends to know a lot and fear nothing."

"That must be difficult for her," Dr. Silverman said.

"It makes her hysterical much of the time," Sunny said. "Although of course she would deny it."

Dr. Silverman nodded.

"And my sister is much like her. She doesn't know much, either, but she substitutes beliefs. She believes in having gone to a good school. She believes in being with a man who's gone to a good school . . . and has prestige . . . and money."

"And that has not worked out for her."

"No, she's gone through husbands and boyfriends and careers without any success in any of them."

"So what she believes hasn't worked for her," Dr. Silverman said.

"God, no," Sunny said. "She doesn't believe in anything real. But her failures have simply made her more entrenched in her silliness. Both of them are, like my father says, often wrong but never uncertain."

"Is she hysterical much of the time as well?"

"Absolutely."

"Would she admit it?" Dr. Silverman said.

"Absolutely not," Sunny said.

They sat quietly. Dr. Silverman was as pulled together as

always: dark skirt, white shirt, very little jewelry, conservative heels. Probably part of the work wardrobe. Don't distract the patient. Her makeup was subtle and quiet. Her nails were manicured and polished.

"They're emotionally disheveled," Sunny said.

Dr. Silverman nodded.

"And they were my role models growing up," Sunny said.

"So you assumed that all women were emotionally disheveled?"

"I didn't want to be like them," Sunny said.

"Who did you want to be like?"

"My father. I don't mean I wanted to be a man. I mean I didn't want to be disheveled."

Dr. Silverman nodded.

"What part did your father play in all this?" she said.

"He took care of them," Sunny said. "Still does. Maybe he enables them, I don't know."

"Why do you suppose he takes care of them?" Dr. Silverman said.

"He's stuck," Sunny said. "He loves them."

"And he loves you," Dr. Silverman said.

"Yes, but he doesn't take care of me."

"Tell me again why your marriage broke up," Dr. Silverman said.

"I guess we were just too different. I mean, my father's a cop. His father's a crook."

"So what drew you to him?"

"He was so complete, and he loved me," she said.

"But Richie wasn't in the family business, you told me."

198

"No," Sunny said. "I believe that he wasn't."

"So why did you break up?"

Sunny sat silently, looking at Dr. Silverman. The question was simple enough. *Why did we break up?* The silence lengthened. Dr. Silverman didn't seem uncomfortable. She simply sat back in her chair and waited. *She trusts me to get this on my own.*

"Jesus Christ," Sunny said.

Dr. Silverman cocked her head and looked attentive.

"It's *because* he's complete," Sunny said. "Because he's like my father, and it made me feel like my mother and sister."

Dr. Silverman smiled. *Good girl,* Sunny said to herself.

"His virtue is his vice," Dr. Silverman said.

ON THE PHONE Liquori said, "I got your message. I guess Ray Mulligan slipped through a crack for a while."

"You know where he is?" Jesse said.

"Not quite," Liquori said. "But I got his parole officer."

"Who might know where he is," Jesse said.

"He's supposed to," Liquori said. "Name's Mark Bloom."

Liquori gave Bloom's phone number to Jesse. Jesse wrote it down.

"You talk to him?" Jesse said.

"Nope, thought you oughta talk to him. It's your case."

"Weren't you up here a little while ago acting like it was your case?" Jesse said.

"That's 'cause Healy asked me," Liquori said.

"And if I asked you?"

"Healy's a state police captain. You ain't," Liquori said. "Hell, Jesse, I'm giving you the parole officer."

"Yeah," Jesse said. "Good. I'll call him."

He hung up.

"For crissake," he said to the empty office, "I'm the chief of police."

Then he dialed the number of Ray Mulligan's parole officer.

"Until a couple weeks ago he lived in your town," Bloom said. "Now he's got a one-roomer in Salem on Lafayette Street. Up toward the college."

"You know why he moved?" Jesse said.

"Worked on an estate on Paradise Neck," Bloom said. "And lived there in a guesthouse. Couple weeks ago they fired him and he had to move out."

"Know the people he worked for?"

"Family named Moynihan," Bloom said.

"What kind of work did he do?"

"Chauffeur," Bloom said.

Jesse snorted quietly on the phone.

"Know why they fired him?" he said.

"Told me he thought the wife had it in for him," Bloom said.

"Say why?"

"Claimed he didn't know."

"What's he doing now?" Jesse said.

"Living off severance pay, looking for work. Severance was generous," Bloom said.

"How much did he get?" Jesse said.

"Enough," Bloom said.

"How much?"

"I'm sorry, Chief, unless it's clearly germane to your case, I feel that is confidential between me and my parolee."

"Your parolee," Jesse said.

"Yes," Bloom said. "He's served his time. He now deserves the same consideration as anyone else."

"You take your job seriously," Jesse said.

"I do. My first responsibility is to protect the public, and my second is to help the parolee."

"Ever a conflict?" Jesse said.

"Of course," Bloom said. "I deal with it on a case-by-case basis."

"Good for you," Jesse said. "I'll need to talk with him."

"Okay," Bloom said.

He gave Jesse the phone number.

"I'll need to talk with him in person," Jesse said.

Bloom gave Jesse the address.

"I'll meet you out front," Bloom said.

"No," Jesse said. "Thanks. I'll need to talk with him alone."

"How come," Bloom said.

"I may need him to tell me things that will get him in trouble with you."

"Like what?"

"I don't want to get him in trouble with you," Jesse said.

"I'm in charge of him," Bloom said. "I'm supposed to know what's going on."

"Not this time," Jesse said.

"What the hell is this?" Bloom said. "I am responsible for the safety of the public."

"And I'm not?" Jesse said.

"Well, yeah," Bloom said. "But I'm supposed to know."

"I feel your pain," Jesse said. "I am the chief of police in Paradise, Massachusetts. I am investigating two murders and I don't know anything."

"It'll go easier if I'm there," Bloom said.

Jesse took in a long breath.

"He won't talk to me if he's worrying about you revoking him right back into Slam City," Jesse said.

"If I send you to him and don't go with you, it'll make me look bad," Bloom said.

Jesse leaned back in his chair and swiveled around so he could look out his office window at the fire trucks being washed in the driveway next door. He breathed in and out carefully.

Then he said, "If you come near me or him while I need him, I will throw your ass out into Lafayette Street and step on your face."

"Hey," Bloom said.

"I will then get you fired," Jesse said.

He hung up the phone and yelled out his office door for Molly. In a moment she appeared.

"Intercom broken?" she said.

"Where's Suit?" Jesse said.

"I believe he is in the squad room drinking coffee."

"Get him in here," Jesse said.

"Wow, are we surly today," Molly said, "or what?"

"Chief-of-police manual allots an hour of surliness a month," Jesse said.

Molly smiled.

"I thought you'd already used up this month's," she said.

"Just get Suit for me," Jesse said.

"I will."

51

L AFAYETTE STREET IN SALEM was lined with substantial clapboard homes and an occasional brick building that had the look of the 1930s. One of them, located on the left-hand side of the street, a little north of the college, was the new home of Ray Mulligan. Jesse was driving his own car, and neither he nor Simpson wore a uniform. They parked across the street.

"Okay," Jesse said. "Mulligan is on the fourth floor, apartment four-B. I'll go in. You wait outside, and make sure no one else enters the apartment."

"What if they insist?"

"Insist back," Jesse said.

"I'm not sure we got any jurisdiction in Salem, do we?"

"If it comes up," Jesse said, "tell 'em we do. I want to talk with Mulligan alone."

"What if there's trouble inside?" Suit said.

"If I scream," Jesse said, "come running. Otherwise, I just want to keep the parole jerk away from us."

Suit saluted.

"Okay, boss," he said.

There was no elevator. They walked up. On the fourth floor they paused to breathe. Then Suit leaned on the wall at the head of the stairs and Jesse walked down the short corridor and knocked on 4B.

Mulligan was big. He was wearing a white tank top and gray sweatpants. He was bald, with a round, red face. He was developing a potbelly, Jesse noticed. His arms were pale and muscular, with some dark prison tattoos. Jesse held up his badge. Mulligan looked at it and smiled.

"I woulda known anyway," he said.

"How?"

"You look like a cop," he said.

"Damn," Jesse said.

Mulligan stepped away from the door, and Jesse went into the apartment. It was very small: a bedroom/sitting room, a kitchenette, and a bath. And it was neat. The bed was made. No clothes lying around. A copy of *The Boston Globe* and one of the *Salem Evening News* were folded on the bed.

"I'm making breakfast," Mulligan said. "Mind if I cook while we talk?"

"Fine," Jesse said. "What are you having?"

"Eggs and spinach," Mulligan said, and went to the stove.

He was wearing brown leather sandals. "What kinda cop are you? I didn't even read the badge."

"My name's Jesse Stone. I'm chief in Paradise."

"Oh, yeah," Mulligan said. "About Knocko getting bopped?"

"Yep."

"Had nothing to do with it," Mulligan said.

"Can you prove it?" Jesse said.

Mulligan stirred the spinach in his fry pan a little with a spatula.

"Don't have to," he said.

"True, but it would save me wasting time if you had an alibi," Jesse said.

"Don't even know exactly when he got bopped," Mulligan said.

Jesse told him.

"Can't remember at the moment," Mulligan said. "But if I need one, I'll bet I can come up with one."

"I'll bet," Jesse said. "You knew Knocko most of your life?"

"Yep, since the first grade, with the nuns, at Saint Anthony's."

"And you were his bodyguard a long time," Jesse said.

"Knocko and me looked out for each other most of our lives."

"Long time."

"He was getting a little soft, last few years." Mulligan patted his belly. "Like most of us. But he was a tough cookie."

"So I've heard."

"He hadn't fired me, maybe I coulda prevented it," Mulligan said.

"Too bad," Jesse said. "Why'd he fire you?"

Mulligan broke two eggs into the fry pan and put the cover on. He looked at the clock on the stove.

"The wife," Mulligan said.

"She fired you?"

Mulligan was timing his eggs.

"Knocko calls me in one morning, and he says, right outta the blue, he says, 'Ray, I gotta let you go.' And I say, 'You're firing me?' And Knocko says, 'Yes. I want you gone today.' And I say, 'Why?' And he says, 'Because I don't want to kill you. I known you too long.'"

Mulligan took the cover off his fry pan and looked at his eggs. He nodded to himself and shut off the stove. With the spatula he carefully slipped the eggs and spinach onto a plate. He put the plate on his little counter and looked at Jesse.

"I say, 'Why would you kill me?' And Knocko says, 'Robbie told me about you. She told me what you were trying on her.' And I say, 'I don't know what you're talking about. I never touched her.' And Knocko says, 'She told me herself. You saying my wife's a liar?' And I say, 'Knocko, on my mother, I never came near her.' And he stands up and he's got a piece and he says, 'Get outta here now, or I swear to God I'll kill you where you stand.' And I know he means it, so I leave. And I ain't never seen him again."

"You mess with the wife?" Jesse said.

"I did not," Mulligan said.

He sat at his counter.

"You mind if I eat?" he said.

"No," Jesse said. "Go ahead, eat."

Mulligan shook salt and pepper onto his eggs.

"The wife mess with you?" Jesse said.

Mulligan had a mouthful of eggs and spinach. He raised his head and nodded approval.

When he had chewed and swallowed, he said, "You're pretty good. Yeah, her and her hot-pants sister, they both came on to me."

"Together or separately?" Jesse said.

"Both," Mulligan said. "You want some coffee?"

"No," Jesse said. "Thanks. But you didn't take the offer?"

"No."

"Because of Knocko?"

"Yeah," Mulligan said. "A'course."

Jesse nodded.

"You think they got you fired so somebody could kill Knocko?"

Mulligan swallowed again and patted his mouth with a paper towel.

"Yeah," he said.

"You know who killed him?" Jesse said.

"Nope, but I know it's got something to do with them two sisters. They'd fuck a haddock if they could get it to hold still."

"Think they messed with Petrov Ognowski?"

"Yeah, sure. I don't know it. But Bob Davis told me they tried him."

"Reggie's bodyguard?"

"Yeah. Don't let Bobby fool you," Mulligan said. "He's not big and mean-looking like me, but. . . ."

"I picked that up," Jesse said.

"Yeah, there's something about Bobby," Mulligan said. "You got it, too."

"That's 'cause I'm the chief of police," Jesse said.

Mulligan grinned.

"No," he said. "It ain't."

Jesse nodded.

"Know why anyone would kill Ognowski?" he said.

"No."

"Knocko?" Jesse said.

"Aside from what I told you about the sisters? No."

"Knocko love his wife?" Jesse said.

"Yeah. Always said he couldn't get over that she married him."

"He get along with Reggie?" Jesse said.

"Far as I know, they was thick as thieves, you pardon the expression."

"You ever think of revenge?"

"On the twin bitches? You're a cop," Mulligan said. "I tell you yes, and something happens to them, who you gonna come see?"

Jesse smiled.

"Come see you anyway," he said.

Mulligan shrugged.

"My parole geek know you're here?" he said.

"Yes."

"He know why?" Mulligan said.

"Just that I wanted to ask you some questions. He wanted to come with me."

"What'd you say?"

"I told him if he showed up here I'd throw him into the middle of Lafayette Street and step on his face."

"Excellent," Mulligan said.

"Anything you haven't told me?"

"Pretty much all I know," Mulligan said.

He ate some toast. Jesse stood and took a card out of his shirt pocket and put it on the counter beside Mulligan.

"Think of anything," Jesse said, "call me."

"Sure," Mulligan said.

"I won't tell your parole officer what we discussed."

"Thanks," Mulligan said.

"But you try to even things up, and something happens to anybody in the case, I'll be back and I'll bring trouble."

Mulligan nodded again.

"You know," he said, "guy like me ain't got much else but trying to keep things even."

"It's trouble you don't need," Jesse said. "I'll even it up."

Mulligan nodded slowly.

"Knew Knocko all my life," he said.

Y OU GOT that kid back to the Renewal folks?" Jesse said.

"Yes," Sunny said.

"She okay?"

"I think so," Sunny said. "Physically, she's fine. I got my doctor to examine her."

"She's happy to be back with the Renewals?"

"Seems so," Sunny said.

"Nice work," Jesse said.

"I hope," Sunny said. "You know what's sweet? I stopped by to check on her, and she told me that Spike comes by once or twice a week to see that she's okay."

"Should make her feel secure," Jesse said.

Sunny nodded. She sat with Jesse on his little balcony in the dark velvet evening, with a glass of white wine. He was nursing a beer. Below them the harbor was dark except for the bob of an occasional light where someone was living on their boat.

"Thing 'bout a view," Jesse said, "is you buy a place for the view and you love it for a couple of days, and then you don't much notice anymore."

"You're noticing now," Sunny said.

"I'm with you," Jesse said.

"And that makes a difference?"

"Yes."

They were quiet. There was remote ambient sound: from the harbor, the faint sound of rigging slapping against mast; from Front Street, an occasional car going by; from the condominium complex, the muffled sound of a television set.

"Thank you," Sunny said.

"You're welcome."

They were sitting side by side. Jesse felt her beside him more insistently than he could remember feeling. The silence of the harbor-front night seemed right. It was as if something exciting might be teetering on the edge. Jesse didn't want to interrupt it.

"I want to tell you about my talk with Dr. Silverman yesterday," Sunny said.

"Okay," Jesse said.

She told him. He listened without a word until she was done.

Then he said, "That's what killed the marriage with Richie. He was too good?"

"Like my father," Sunny said. "And I was afraid I'd turn into a dependent mess, like my mother and my sister."

Jesse nodded.

"Well, for what it's worth," he said. "You didn't."

"I feared it," Sunny said. "I fought him every day, his goodness. I competed with him every day. I was fighting for my life."

"Not to be your mother."

"Yes."

"His flaw was he was so good?" Jesse said.

"In a manner of speaking," Sunny said, "yes."

"No wonder you like me," Jesse said.

"I do like you," Sunny said.

"Good," Jesse said. "I'll try not to improve."

"Stop fishing for compliments," Sunny said. "I think much more highly of you than you think of yourself."

"A divorced small-town cop with a drinking problem," Jesse said. "And no future."

"Take that up with Dix," Sunny said. "I've sort of broken out, and I'm thrilled, and I'm not going to be shanghaied into your pathologies."

"Oh," Jesse said.

"I am freed of a burden I've carried all my life," Sunny said.

"I know," Jesse said. "Good for you."

"She's a good shrink," Sunny said.

"Gotta have both," Jesse said. "Good shrink, good patient."

"Thank you."

"You're welcome."

"How are you doing with the double murder," Sunny said.

"Good news/bad news," Jesse said. "I'm pretty sure how most of it went down, and I can't prove any of it."

"Knowing is good," Sunny said.

"Proving is better."

He told her what he knew.

"And not a fact to take to the DA," Sunny said.

"No," Jesse said. "But I do have two dangerous men circling the scene, looking for revenge."

"You think they're serious."

"Absolutely," Jesse said. "And worse than that, they're probably pretty good at it."

"You're pretty good, too," Sunny said.

Jesse shrugged.

"I misjudged those two women completely," he said. "They were beautiful, poised, completely devoted to their husbands. Hell, I was half in love with them myself."

"Things are not always what they seem," Sunny said.

"God, you sound like Dix," Jesse said.

"That was shrinky," Sunny said. "Wasn't it."

"It was."

"Have you talked with Dix," Sunny said, "about why you were so taken?"

"I have," Jesse said.

"You want to share?" Sunny said.

Jesse nodded.

"Yes," he said. "But I need to take some time with it."

"Later?"

"When I've got my murder case cleared," Jesse said.

"I look forward," Sunny said.

He finished his beer and put the bottle down. They sat for a while and listened to the silence.

"I gotta ask you something," Jesse said.

"Of course," Sunny said.

She put her empty wineglass on the table beside his empty beer bottle.

"Your psychological breakthrough," Jesse said. "Do you suppose it will affect our relationship?"

"Why, Jesse," Sunny said. "I didn't know you cared."

"I do," Jesse said.

"I'm teasing," Sunny said. "I know you do."

"So?" Jesse said. "Effect?"

"I should think it would have a good effect," Sunny said. "But it always takes two to tango."

"I know," Jesse said.

"What effect do you think it will have?" Sunny said.

"Don't know yet," Jesse said. "But I'm hopeful. If it helps you move on from Richie . . ."

"It will," Sunny said. "How about you. Have you really moved on from Jenn?"

"I think so, don't you?"

"I think so, but I'd still like to know what Dix thinks about you and the Bang Bang Twins."

"I need to get it organized in my own head," Jesse said. "Is sexual intercourse acceptable in the meantime?"

"It is," Sunny said.

"Oh, good," Jesse said.

Sunny stood up and smiled at him.

"Enough with the love talk," she said. "Off with the clothes."

53

DRIVING BACK TO BOSTON, Sunny thought about Jesse and herself. He was certainly someone she liked, maybe more than liked. He was funny and kind and a very good cop. And in the privacy of her car she admitted to herself that his flaws were probably an asset. He had a drinking problem. He'd been fired in Los Angeles. His marriage had failed. She was pretty sure he could control the drinking; she'd seen him do it. The rest was really water under the bridge, but it made her feel less endangered—she smiled at her own word—less likely to be overpowered. . . . If he could control the drinking . . . and not her. . . . Did he want to control her? Not exactly . . . It was more that she was supposed to be a certain way . . . look a certain way . . . something like that . . . and with her new insight, she could probably prevent herself from being controlled, anyway . . . or whatever it was.

She had crossed the General Edwards Bridge and was approaching Wonderland when her cell phone rang.

"Sunny, it's Spike. You need to come to the Gray Gull, now."

"Why?"

"Cheryl is here," Spike said. "There's something a little wrong at the Bond of the Renewal."

"I'm in Revere," Sunny said.

"Turn around," Spike said.

"Cheryl all right?"

"She's with me," Spike said. "She's starting to calm down."

"So, what is it?" Sunny said.

"Sex," Spike said. "I think. She's a little incoherent."

"Okay," Sunny said. "I'm on my way."

She had reached Bell Circle, and turned back.

THE GRAY GULL didn't open until noon, and when Sunny went in there was only Spike and Cheryl sitting at the bar. There was a plate of scrambled eggs and toast on the bar beside Cheryl. She appeared not to have touched them. There was a mug of coffee, from which she drank. Spike had coffee, too. When Sunny came in, Spike pointed at his coffee and raised his eyebrows. Sunny shook her head. She sat on a bar stool on the other side of Cheryl.

"What's up," Sunny said.

Cheryl started to cry.

"Perhaps I should rephrase," Sunny said.

Cheryl shook her head and kept crying.

"What's going to happen to me," she said. "Where can I go?"

"You don't have to go anywhere," Spike said. "You can stay right here."

"I can't . . ." Cheryl paused and cried harder, and got it a little under control and tried again. "I can't go home. I can't stay in the Renewal House."

"Why?" Sunny said.

"They want me to fuck a bunch of old guys," Cheryl said.

"All at once?" Sunny said.

"No."

"When you say they want you to," Sunny said, "how insistent are they."

"They say I have to."

"And 'they' are who?" Sunny said.

"The Patriarch and the Seniors."

"Seniors?"

"The, like, discipline board, you know?" Cheryl said. "Like, the oldest people in the Bond."

"And why do they want you to fuck a bunch of old guys?" Sunny said.

"It's, like, a reward," Cheryl said. "They have a big party and the old guys give money to the Bond, and the Bond gives them a girl."

"A goddamned fund-raiser?" Sunny said.

Spike nodded.

"Did you know about this when I brought you back?" Sunny said.

"I knew that sometimes they had these parties and some of the girls went with some of the men," Cheryl said. "But I thought it was because they wanted to."

"But it was forced?" Sunny said.

"They said if I didn't, I'd be booted out of the Bond."

"Are other girls in the same boat?" Sunny said.

"Yes," Cheryl said.

"Probably used the ones who had no other options," Spike said.

Sunny nodded.

"So, did you do it?" Sunny said.

"Yes," Cheryl said. "I mean, it's not like I'm a virgin, but an old fat guy I never even met before?"

"You had sex with this guy at the Renewal House?" Sunny said.

Cheryl nodded.

"And as soon as it was over," she said, "I just put my clothes on and ran out of the house and ran here."

"You did the right thing," Sunny said.

"But where can I go?" Cheryl said.

"Here," Spike said. "You can stay with me while we work things out."

"You?" Cheryl said.

"I won't molest you," Spike said. "I'm gayer than a French polka."

"I guess so," Cheryl said.

"We'll figure something out," Sunny said. "Let me look into it all a little more."

"You won't tell them where I am," Cheryl said.

"No, but even if I did, Spike won't let anyone bother you," Sunny said.

"Even if there was a lot of them?"

"Even if the whole board of Seniors came," Spike said.

"You may recall Spike in action," Sunny said, "when we got you out of the Rackley center."

Cheryl looked at Spike.

"I think you beat up about three or four people," she said. "It's kind of hard to remember."

"Three," Spike said. "Piece of cake."

Sunny stood.

"What are you going to do?" Cheryl said.

"I'm not sure yet," Sunny said. "I may consult with the local chief of police."

"Weren't you consulting with him last night?" Spike said.

"I was," Sunny said.

"Probably good I didn't call till this morning," Spike said.

"It was," Sunny said. "I think my cell phone was turned off."

"Unlike yourself," Spike said.

"Bite your tongue," Sunny said.

She looked at Cheryl.

"You okay?" Sunny said. "You need a bath, a doctor, anything?"

"I took a shower," Cheryl said. "And Spike put my clothes

through his washer/dryer. But I don't have any of my other stuff."

"Okay," Sunny said. "I'll get your stuff."

"What if they won't give it to you," Cheryl said.

Sunny smiled.

"I'll get your stuff," she said.

54

MOLLY BROUGHT Natalya Ognowski into Jesse's office and held a chair for her to sit. Jesse could smell her perfume as she came in the door. *Lotta perfume.* She sat with her feet in their high pink wedges flat on the floor and her knees pressed together modestly. She was wearing a skirt that barely reached her thighs and a very tight cropped pink T-shirt that showed a lot of waistline. Her waist looked a little soft to Jesse, but he had recently been looking at Sunny Randall, whose waistline was not soft. Natalya was carrying a large straw bag that matched her T-shirt. She looked up timidly at Jesse.

"Chief Stone?" she said.

"Jesse," he said. "It's Natalya, isn't it?"

She nodded.

"Natalya Ognowski," she said.

"Nice to see you again, Natalya."

"Thank you," she said. "I need to talk about something."

"Good," Jesse said.

"I need your advice."

"You would be unusual in that," Jesse said.

"Excuse me?"

"I'll be glad to give you my advice," Jesse said.

"I have been dating Mr. Normie Salerno," she said.

Jesse leaned back in his chair and folded his hands across his stomach.

"Muscleman? Works for Reggie Galen?"

"Yes."

"Really?" Jesse said.

"Yes," Natalya said. "I am trying to find out who killed my husband."

"You are?"

"Yes," Natalya said.

"Does he know who you are?"

"No. He thinks I am a girl he picked up at the bar at Gray Gull."

"Why him?" Jesse said.

"He was who I could pick up," Natalya said.

Jesse looked at her silently for a moment.

"I'll be damned," he said. "Do you like him?"

"No," Natalya said. "He is a pig."

"I didn't like him much when I met him," Jesse said.

"But I date him and we do sex, and I give him vodka, and he talks about himself. But he doesn't talk about what I want to know. So we do more sex and I give him more vodka. I drink some of the vodka, too."

"I don't blame you," Jesse said.

"It is not so bad, I have only to give him sex and pretend I like it, and I can ask him about himself and he talks. He is very boring, but it is better than always doing sex."

Jesse was quiet. He knew she would tell her story in the way that she would tell it. There was no point hurrying her. If she had something, it would eventually appear.

"We always go to my apartment," she said. "I say I am only comfortable there. And he does not care where we do it. I am very good at doing sex."

Jesse smiled and nodded.

"And I have a tape machine that listens to everything that is said."

She took a small tape recorder out of her purse and put it on the edge of Jesse's desk in front of her. Jesse raised his eyebrows.

"Is it all right if I play some of it?" she said.

"It is," Jesse said.

"I will only play a part I think is important. Much of all the tape I have is of us doing sex, or Normie talking dirty. And me talking dirty to him to make him like me. It is embarrassing. I do not wish to play that."

"Good," Jesse said.

"Will you plug it in, please," Natalya said. "I do not know if the batteries are lasting."

Jesse plugged it in. Natalya stood and hovered over the machine for a moment. Then she pushed play and sat back down in her chair.

"*We do all these things,*" Natalya said. "*And I do not even know your whole name.*"

"*Norman Anthony Salerno,*" he said.

Jesse was watching Natalya. She was listening as if she'd never heard it before.

Natalya giggled on the tape.

"*How come you have such big muscles, Norman Anthony Salerno?*"

There was a faint sound of ice cubes clicking in a glass.

"*I pump a lot of iron,*" he said. "*It's useful in my line of work.*"

"*What do you do for work,*" Natalya said.

"*I fuck you,*" he said, and laughed.

The ice cubes clicked again.

Natalya showed nothing as the tape ran. Occasionally she looked at Jesse, as if she wanted his approval.

"*You don't need big muscles for that,*" Natalya said. "*What do you do for money?*"

"*Man, you broads are all the same,*" he said. "*'What do you do for money?' I got plenty of money, don't worry about that.*"

"*So, where you get plenty of money?*"

The ice clinked.

"*I'm the head of security for a very rich man,*" he said.

"*Is that dangerous?*"

"*Can be,*" Normie said.

"*You have a gun?*"

"*Sure,*" he said. "*Guy my size don't usually need one, but now and then you need one, you know? To take care of business.*"

"*What is 'take care of business'?*"

Normie laughed.

"*Man, you don't know much, do you,*" he said.

"*No,*" she said.

"*If somebody's a problem, and he has to be whacked . . . I take care of business.*"

"*'Whacked'?*" she said.

"*For crissake, killed,*" Normie said. "*You understand killed?*"

"*You kill people?*"

"*I've killed a few,*" Normie said. "*Get me a drink.*"

There was the sound of bedsprings and a faint sound of bottles and glasses and ice, then the bedspring sound again.

"*Have you actually kill somebody?*" Natalya said.

"*Sure.*"

"*I don't believe that,*" Natalya said. "*I believe you tough guy. But I don't believe you kill someone.*"

"*No?*"

"*No.*"

"*I kill someone, two someones, right in town,*" he said.

"*In Paradise?*"

"*Absolutely,*" Normie said. "*You probably read about it in the papers.*"

"*The two men on Paradise Neck?*"

"*Bingo,*" Normie said.

"*I do not believe that,*" Natalya said.

"*Ognowski,*" Normie said, "*and Moynihan.*"

"*You really did?*" she said.

"*Bet your ass,*" Normie said. "*Course, you tell anybody and I'll deny it.*"

There was the sound of ice and glass and the faint sound of swallowing.

"*And I'll kill you.*"

"I will not tell," Natalya said.

"I'll bet you won't," he said.

Again, the sound of drinking.

Then he said, *"Let's get back to business here."*

She giggled.

"You like how many times I can go?" he said.

"Of course," she said.

"Pretty good, huh?" he said.

"Very good," she said.

55

NATALYA LEANED forward and stopped the tape.

"It is embarrassing," she said.

"I'll need to hear it all," Jesse said.

She nodded.

"When I am gone," she said. "It is embarrassing to listen to it."

"Yes," Jesse said.

"Is he caught?" Natalya said.

"You have caught him," Jesse said.

"Good, then I will not have to see him again."

"You will probably have to testify," Jesse said.

She nodded.

"He killed Petrov Ognowski," she said. "My husband. Nicolas Ognowski's son."

Jesse nodded.

"He will not go to trial," she said.

"One of you will kill him?" Jesse said.

"Yes."

"Why did you bring this to me?" Jesse said.

"To be sure," Natalya said. "If somehow he is not killed, you will know. My father-in-law says you are good cop. You would find a way to get him."

"If he is killed," Jesse said, "I'm going to have to come looking for you."

"Of course," Natalya said. "But you will not find us."

"The thing is," Jesse said, "Normie is a nobody. He would have no reason to kill either of those people unless he were told to by Reggie Galen. In fact, he wouldn't dare unless he were told to."

"You think Normie is lying?"

"He might be," Jesse said.

"To impress me?"

"Maybe," Jesse said.

"So maybe I find out who did it and I am wrong?" she said.

"Usually that kind of work for Reggie Galen would be done by a man named Bob Davis."

"So I have failed?"

"No," Jesse said. "You've done a great job. That tape gives me enough leverage on Normie to flip him."

" 'Flip'?"

"Get him to testify for our side, make him a deal."

"So he get away with it?" Natalya said.

"No, he'll do time," Jesse said.

"Not enough," Natalya said.

"We flip him and we can probably roll up everybody involved. He's a blow. Once I've got him, he'll talk to me about everything."

"My father-in-law can do that," Natalya said.

"I'm sure he can," Jesse said. "But with somebody's foot on his neck, how do you know he's telling the truth?"

"How will you?"

"We'll gather evidence."

Natalya leaned back in her chair and crossed her legs and tapped her fingertips together in front of her face.

"Who is this man, Bob Davis."

"Reggie Galen's bodyguard, last I knew," Jesse said. "He's not Normie."

"No?"

"No," Jesse said. "I'm pretty sure he's the real deal."

"You think he kill my husband?"

"I don't know, but let me find out. Otherwise, you could end up killing the wrong man."

"My father-in-law does not care if he kills somebody wrong," she said.

"But you both care," Jesse said, "about killing the right guy."

"Yes."

"If you kill Normie, you may eliminate our only chance to be sure who the right guy is," Jesse said.

"You don't think Normie is the right guy?"

"He might be. He might not be. The point is, even if he is the right guy, he isn't the only right guy. Somebody told him to do it."

Natalya nodded.

"Who?" Jesse said. "Why?"

She nodded again.

"I will discuss with my father-in-law," she said, and stood.

Jesse unplugged the little recorder and took the tape and handed the recorder to Natalya.

"I'll need the tape," he said.

Natalya nodded.

"It is a copy," she said.

"One other thing," Jesse said. "Before you go."

Natalya paused in the doorway.

"It is very brave," Jesse said, "and very smart, what you did."

"I loved my husband," she said.

Jesse nodded.

"And somebody killed him," she said.

Jesse nodded again.

"There has to be payment."

"Yes," Jesse said. "And there will be. Just give me enough time to make sure it's payment in full."

"I will discuss it with my father-in-law," she said.

56

SUNNY HAD LUNCH with Jesse at Daisy's Café.

"Did you tell me she originally wanted to name this place Daisy Dyke's?" Sunny said.

"Yeah," Jesse said. "But the town went bonkers. One civil liberties group started picketing the place, contended it was demeaning to dykes."

"But Daisy is a dyke," Sunny said. "Isn't she?"

"Yep, and none of the picketers were."

"I notice you always call it Daisy Dyke's?" Sunny said.

"Yep," Jesse said.

"Are you just being recalcitrant?" Sunny said.

"Probably," Jesse said. "But she calls herself Daisy Dyke. I think I'm respecting her wishes."

The waitress arrived with menus.

"Special today is strawberry pie. Bread is anadama. We got a lobster, tomato, and lettuce sandwich that's not on the menu," she said. "And the iced tea is mango. You want a minute?"

"Nope," Sunny said. "I can do it."

They ordered.

"I'm buying," Sunny said.

"Good."

"I want to talk about something, sort of off the record," Sunny said.

"What record?" Jesse said.

"Never mind," Sunny said. "What I really want, probably, is advice."

"You, too?" Jesse said.

"What do you mean, me, too?"

"I'll tell you about it later," Jesse said. "Whaddya got?"

"There's something nasty going on at the Bond of the Renewal," Sunny said.

"What?" Jesse said.

Sunny told him about it. During the telling the waitress came and poured them iced tea from a large round pitcher. Jesse drank some as he listened.

"The kid's with Spike," Jesse said.

"Yes."

"She should be safe there," Jesse said.

"Unless someone has an elephant gun," Sunny said.

"It is possible to acquire an elephant gun," Jesse said.

"But unlikely at the Renewal House," Sunny said.

"Anyway, you need any help looking out for her, let me know."

"Thank you," Sunny said. "Now, what are we going to do about the Bond of the Renewal?"

The waitress brought lunch. Jesse had the lobster sandwich. Sunny had a salad. Jesse's iced tea was gone. The waitress refilled his glass.

"Seems to me they're conducting a criminal enterprise," Jesse said.

"Prostitution?"

"Yep, sexual coercion, maybe rape, maybe kidnapping," Jesse said. "I'd say they are in trouble."

"If she testifies," Sunny said.

"And you think testifying would be hard on her," Jesse said.

"Yes."

"Probably some other folks we could get to testify instead," Jesse said. "How would you like to handle this?"

"There are a couple of ways," Sunny said. "One would be I go up there with Spike and admonish them."

"I fear felonious assault," Jesse said.

"Yes, that is a danger," Sunny said. "The other way is that I go talk to them, and I keep the Paradise police informed, and we see what develops."

"With an eye to protecting the kid as much as we can," Jesse said.

"Cheryl," Sunny said. "Yes. Okay with you?"

"The Paradise Police Department has a pretty full plate at

the moment," Jesse said. "I'm grateful for the help. I'll tell Molly about it, and ask her to be, ah, liaison with you."

The waitress cleared their lunch dishes, poured Jesse more iced tea, and said, "Dessert?"

"I need that strawberry pie," Jesse said.

"Sure, Jesse," the waitress said. "You, ma'am?"

"No, thank you," Sunny said.

"Two forks?" the waitress said.

"No," Jesse said.

AFTER LUNCH they walked back to the station, where Sunny had parked. It was late summer, and cooler than it usually was in August. The sky seemed clean and fresh, and the air was soft. The houses of the old town were built intimately next to each other and to the street. There were a lot of people walking around.

"You never told me who else was asking advice," Sunny said.

Jesse told her. By the time he finished they had reached the police station and were leaning on Sunny's car in the parking lot.

"Wow," Sunny said. "That's some woman."

"You'd be even more impressed with her fortitude," Jesse said, "if you knew Normie."

"Have you listened to the tape?"

"The one she left, and five more she sent over," Jesse said.

"How was that?"

"Awful," Jesse said. "A lot of Normie talking about what a stud he was. A lot of sound effects from them having carnal knowledge."

"Ugh," Sunny said.

"Think how it was for her," Jesse said. "But she never let on."

"You think she might kill him?" Sunny said.

"She might," Jesse said. "Ognowski's father might. Ray Mulligan might, if he knew."

"You do have a full plate," Sunny said.

"I do."

"Do you have a plan?" she said.

"I'll talk to the DA," Jesse said. "But I'd say I have enough to arrest Normie. Even if I don't, I can bring him in and play the tapes for him."

"And if you're lucky, he'll die of embarrassment," Sunny said.

"And of course there's still the Bang Bang Twins," Jesse said.

"You say Normie was a bodybuilder?" Sunny said.

"Big-time," Jesse said.

"My knowledge of them is secondhand," Sunny said. "But it certainly seems possible that the twins might have played their game with a healthy young muscleman."

"Or a strapping thug like Petrov Ognowski," Jesse said.

"They played it with you," Sunny said.

"Who can blame them for that," Jesse said.

"Not me," Sunny said. "You have anything else to do?"

"I'm going to see if I can find Bob Davis," Jesse said.

"Will you do something for me?" Sunny said. "Will you run Jarrod Russell for me?"

"Sure," Jesse said. "Who's he?"

"The Patriarch of the Bond of the Renewal."

"Jarrod Russell," Jesse said.

Sunny nodded and leaned forward and kissed Jesse on the mouth. Jesse kissed her back. They embraced. Then each leaned away without releasing the other.

"Good luck," Sunny said.

Jesse patted her on the backside.

"To us both," he said.

58

WEARING PINK-AND-WHITE sneakers in case she needed to move quickly, and white shorts and a pink tank top to go with the sneakers, Sunny went to visit the Bond of the Renewal. She carried a white shoulder bag in which was lip gloss, a wallet, and a short-barreled revolver.

The Patriarch received her in the Renewal office, with a view of the harbor. He was wearing the same kind of white linen he'd worn when she'd seen him before. Must be his Patriarch uniform. He gestured for her to take a seat. She shook her head.

"I've come to pick up Cheryl DeMarco's stuff," she said.

The Patriarch blinked.

"Cheryl?" he said.

"Cheryl DeMarco," Sunny said.

"Cheryl has run off," the Patriarch said.

"Yes, she has," Sunny said. "And she wants me to pick up her stuff."

The Patriarch leaned back in his chair. It was a good chair, ergonomic in design.

"I'm sorry, Ms. Randall," he said. "But Cheryl DeMarco's stuff belongs to Cheryl DeMarco. It is not mine to give, nor yours to take."

"Wow," Sunny said.

"Excuse me?"

"You're good," she said.

"I'm afraid I don't understand," the Patriarch said.

"You truly sound like a kind man concerned with the individual rights of your people," Sunny said.

"Yes," the Patriarch said.

"But you are actually a man who will prostitute out young girls for money."

Sunny watched as the pinkness faded from the Patriarch's face, and his hair and face became the same color. It didn't improve his appearance.

"What . . ." He seemed to be trying to catch his breath. "What . . . are you . . . saying?"

"I'm saying you're a pimp," Sunny said. "And I want Cheryl's stuff down here in one minute or I'm calling the cops."

"No," the Patriarch said. "No. Wait."

His voice had grown hoarse. Sunny held her arm out and looked at her wristwatch.

"No, we'll get them right away. Just wait a minute. I'll have someone get them right now."

Sunny nodded and continued to look at her watch. The Patriarch picked up the phone and punched a button.

"Darlene," he said. "This is an emergency. Get a couple of the girls to go to Cheryl DeMarco's room and pack everything up and bring it to my office."

He paused, listening.

"Use whatever is necessary," he said. "Suitcase, plastic bag, whatever, just hurry up."

He hung up the phone.

"It will be here very soon," he said.

Sunny stopped looking at her watch and stood where she had stood since she came in, at an angle to the desk so that she could see the Patriarch but also see the door to the office.

"But we have to talk. We have to make some arrangement," he said. "First of all, no such thing has ever happened. In fact, I categorically deny everything."

"Categorically," Sunny said.

He shook his head as if there was something in his ear.

"Who on earth," he said, "has told you such a terrible thing?"

Sunny shook her head sadly.

"Jarrod," she said. "Jarrod. Don't any of you jerks ever learn? What gets you in trouble, remember, is not so much the crime, it's the damn cover-up."

"You called me Jarrod," he said.

"I feel that I know you," Sunny said.

"I prefer to be called Patriarch," he said.

"Frankly, Jarrod," Sunny said, "I don't give a rat's ass."

The Patriarch blinked again.

"What are you going to do?" he said.

"When your minions bring it to me," Sunny said, "I'm going to take Cheryl's stuff and leave."

Blink.

"Are you . . ." he said. "What are you . . . Are you going to cause trouble?"

"Oh, absolutely," Sunny said.

Two blinks.

"Surely," he said, "we can work something out."

The door opened and a short woman in jeans and a T-shirt came in carrying a black plastic trash bag. She looked at the Patriarch. He nodded, and the woman put the bag in front of the desk and backed out of the room.

"It would be good if you gave me a list of your principal donors," Sunny said.

"Oh my God," he said, "no. That's privileged information."

" 'Privileged,' " Sunny said, and shook her head. "It should be available in your annual report. Have a copy of that handy?"

"We, ah, don't do an annual report," he said.

"I think you're supposed to," Sunny said. "I'll check with the IRS."

"IRS?"

"You do annual taxes?" Sunny said.

"We're simply a small, private spiritual organization," the Patriarch said.

Sunny picked up the trash bag. It was light. Cheryl didn't seem to have much stuff.

"And whorehouse," Sunny said, and carried the bag out of the office.

59

THIS TIME IT WAS Normie who brought Jesse in to see Reggie. He didn't say anything, but Jesse could feel Normie's attitude like an aura.

Reggie was sitting in the backyard under an awning with a glass of iced coffee. Both the Bang Bang Twins were with him, dressed alike in yellow sundresses. If they had any memory of appearing naked before him, Jesse couldn't detect it. They were as charming and composed as they were before the incident.

"Can I get you some iced coffee, Chief Stone?" one of the twins said.

"Yes," Jesse said. "Thank you."

She went to get it. Jesse looked at the remaining twin.

"Robbie?" he said.

She laughed.

"You had a fifty-fifty chance," she said. "Actually, I'm Rebecca."

"Mrs. Galen," Jesse said.

"Got that right," Reggie said. "I think."

Everybody laughed. Robbie came back with the iced coffee. Jesse added sugar and milk.

"Why I stopped by," Jesse said, "is to inquire after Bob Davis."

"Bobby," Reggie said.

Jesse nodded.

"Damn, I miss him," Reggie said.

"Where is he?" Jesse said.

"Don't know."

"Why isn't he here?" Jesse said.

"He quit," Reggie said. "Told me he wanted to kick back a little. Go to the track, play golf, look at the ocean."

"Golf," Jesse said.

"What he said."

"You have a replacement?" Jesse said.

"Normie Salerno," Reggie said. "For the moment."

"Seems to me that he's no Bob Davis," Jesse said.

"No," Reggie said. "He's not. But he's here until I get somebody else."

"You know where Bob is?"

"Nope."

"No forwarding address?" Jesse said.

"Nope. Told me he wanted a clean break. Shook my hand and"—Reggie shrugged—"went."

"We all miss him," one of the twins said.

"He was sweet," the other twin said.

"Knocko's guy goes," Jesse said. "Then yours."

"Yeah."

"Then Knocko went," Jesse said.

Reggie looked at Jesse in silence for a long time.

Finally he said, "Meaning?"

Jesse made an airy motion with his hand.

"Just reviewing the facts of the situation," he said.

Reggie nodded.

"Well," he said. "If there's nothing else . . ."

"No," Jesse said. "Nothing else. I'll find my way out."

All three of them watched him leave. As he reached the corner of the house, Jesse turned and looked back.

"Watch your back, Reggie," he said.

None of them spoke.

60

JESSE GATHERED the eight women in the Bond of the Renewal in the living room of the Renewal House. Sunny was with him, and Suit, and Molly, and the Patriarch.

"I don't understand," the Patriarch said. "I don't understand why you are doing this."

"I'm investigating a reported felony," Jesse said.

"Do I need a lawyer?"

"You know that better than I do," Jesse said.

"I don't know any lawyers," the Patriarch said.

"If I arrest you," Jesse said, "a lawyer will be provided."

"Arrest?"

The Patriarch was horrified.

"I need to talk to these ladies now, sir," Jesse said. "I'll ask you to join Officer Simpson outside."

The Patriarch hesitated. Suit took his arm, and they left the room. Molly closed the door and leaned against the wall beside it.

"I'm Jesse Stone," he said to the women. "I am the chief of police here in Paradise. The officer by the door is Molly Crane. And the other woman is a private detective from Boston named Sunny Randall, who is working with us."

The eight women looked dutifully at each of the people as Jesse introduced them.

"As you may know," Jesse said, "a member of the Bond, Cheryl DeMarco, has reported to us that she was forced to have sex with one or more of the donors at a fund-raising event here recently."

No one said anything.

"We are not accusing anyone here of any wrongdoing. We have no intention of arresting you or anything unpleasant. We are just trying to establish what has happened here."

All the women looked at him solemnly. One of them, a very young-looking woman with a single long black braid, raised her hand.

Jesse nodded at her.

"Where is Cheryl now?" she said.

"What is your name?" Jesse said.

"Billie."

"She's fine, Billie," Jesse said. "She's staying with a friend."

Billie nodded. No one else spoke.

"What I need to know is was she telling the truth, and have

any of you been required to have sex with a donor, or with any-one else."

No one said anything. No one moved.

"I'm not interested in consensual sex. I'm interested in sex that, had it not been urged on you, you wouldn't have had."

Nothing.

"And I'm not limiting the definition of sex; any of the vari-ety of sexual activities that are available would do."

Billie looked a little uncomfortable, Jesse thought. And an older woman, maybe thirty, in a gauzy white dress, looked down at the floor.

"Okay," Jesse said. "It's kind of embarrassing, isn't it. Might be easier if I left the room."

He looked at Sunny. She nodded. Jesse turned and walked out of the living room and closed the door behind him. He was in the entry hall. At the end of the hall was the patriarchal office, where Suit was standing by the door.

Jesse walked down. The Patriarch was sitting at his desk, looking at his hands.

"How's everything?" Jesse said.

"He's mentioned several times that he doesn't understand what's going on," Suit said.

"And your reply?" Jesse said.

"I told him that was the story of my life," Suit said.

"Consoling," Jesse said.

"What's going on now," the Patriarch said, still staring down at his hands.

"My ladies are talking with your ladies," Jesse said.

"Girl talk," Suit said.

"I think *woman talk* is more correct," Jesse said.

"I'm sure it is," Suit said.

"Why are the women talking?" the Patriarch said.

"We're trying to establish who else you pimped off to your high rollers," Jesse said. "They seemed a little embarrassed in front of me."

"I wish you wouldn't speak that way," the Patriarch said.

"Sure you do," Jesse said.

"I have done nothing," the Patriarch said, "except in the service of simple spiritual values."

"That's true for all of us, I'm sure," Jesse said. "Especially if you see money as a spiritual value."

"Any money I have raised has been in the service of the Renewal."

"I sense that a discussion of ends versus means is about to break out," Jesse said.

"Jesse?" Suit said, and nodded toward the hall.

The living-room door was open, and Molly was standing in the doorway. Jesse looked at her, and she nodded toward the living room behind her. Then she went back in, leaving the door open.

"Make sure Mr. Patriarch stays here," Jesse said to Suit. "We may have a verdict."

He walked down the door and into the living room. The women were seated as they had been before. None looked at Jesse. Molly winked at him. Jesse looked at Sunny.

"Anybody?" he said.

"All of them," Sunny said.

61

J ESSE TOOK HIM into a cell, for dramatic effect. He held the tape recorder in front of the Patriarch and punched it on. Sunny sat on the bunk. Molly leaned against the cell door.

"Please give your name," Jesse said to the Patriarch.

"I am the Patriarch of the Bond of the Renewal," the Patriarch said.

"That's what you do," Jesse said. "I want your name."

"Jarrod Russell."

"Okay," Jesse said. "From here on, we will all refer to you as Jarrod Russell."

"Yes, sir."

Jesse gave the date and location of the interview. Then he shut off the tape recorder.

"We got you, Jarrod," Jesse said. "You know that."

Russell nodded. Then he put his face in his hands and began to cry.

"Every one of those women will testify against you," Jesse said. "Right, Moll?"

"They will," Molly said.

"Every one of them was coerced into sexual activity with donors," Jesse said.

"They were," Sunny said.

"We have statements from all of them," Jesse said.

"We do," Molly said.

"You're going to jail," Jesse said.

Jarrod Russell sobbed into his hands. Everyone else was quiet.

After a time Jesse said, "Unless we can work some kind of deal."

Russell raised his face from his hands. *Salvation?*

"I'll do anything you want," he said.

Jesse was silent for a long time while Russell looked at him. Then he said, "How'd you get yourself into this mess?"

"I founded this little group," Russell said in a thick, shaky voice. "I had some money from my family, and I wanted to do good. And it was good for a while, but eventually . . ."

Jesse waited. Russell seemed to have trouble getting enough air. He took a couple of big inhales.

"I really was happy," he said.

No one said anything.

"But eventually the money ran out, and I started trying to raise money. At first I had the girls making cookies and things. . . .

Then one man offered one of the girls money to have sex with him . . . and she did and gave the money to me . . ."

"Which girl?" Sunny said.

Russell shook his head.

"She has since left us," he said.

"Gone but not forgotten," Sunny said.

Russell dropped his head and nodded. When he spoke, his voice was shaky.

"It was all in the service of good," he said.

"Except when it wasn't," Molly said.

No one said anything. Russell had stopped crying. But his breathing was still shaky. Jesse stood and walked to the cell door and looked into the corridor for a time. Then he turned back toward Russell.

"Okay," Jesse said. "Here's the deal. You tell me who was having sex with your girls, and I'll help you with the DA. Maybe you won't have to do time if you are cooperative."

"If you let me go back to my office," Russell said, "I can give you a list."

MOLLY AND STEVE FRIEDMAN took Russell to his office to
make his list. Jesse and Sunny sat in Jesse's office.

"You played him like a mackerel," Sunny said.

"I know."

"I felt kind of sorry for him," Sunny said.

"I did, too, but that wasn't the time to show it."

"No," Sunny said. "It was a pleasure to watch you work."

"Thank you."

"There is one thing that bothers me a little," Sunny said.

"Which is?"

"You never quite said what crime we got him on."

Jesse smiled and put his finger to his lips.

"*Shhh,*" he said.

"You didn't actually arrest him, did you?" Sunny said.

Jesse shook his head.

"Are you going to?" Sunny said.

"I'll consult with the DA's office," Jesse said. "But something wrong went on there. I'm sure we can come up with a charge if we want to."

"None of the girls wanted to have sex with any of the men," Sunny said.

"If they are telling the truth," Jesse said.

"I think they are," Sunny said. "But I'm not sure the men who had sex with them knew it was involuntary."

"There was an implicit agreement to trade sex for money," Jesse said.

"Which would be prostitution," Sunny said.

"There was coercion," Jesse said.

"Which is rarely admirable," Sunny said. "But not always illegal."

"And at some level, pretty common," Jesse said.

"Oh, God," Sunny said. "Most women have experienced some . . . 'What are you, frigid?' . . . 'What am I supposed to do with these feelings?' And my personal favorite, 'Hey, I bought you dinner. . . .' Like I'm supposed to bop you for a lobster roll?"

"I never used any of those on you," Jesse said.

"You never had to," Sunny said.

"It is my impression that most women are willing these days," Jesse said.

"I think that's true," Sunny said.

"I doubt that there were many virgins working for the donors' dollars," Jesse said.

"I think that's probably true also," Sunny said. "But . . ."

Jesse nodded.

"If you don't want to, you shouldn't have to," he said.

"Whether you're a virgin or a whore," Sunny said.

Jesse nodded.

"On the other hand," he said, "didn't I buy you dinner the other night?"

"Oh, oink," Sunny said. "What are you going to do now?"

"I'll buy you dinner again," Jesse said. "I'm not a quitter."

"I meant with Russell and the Renewal and all that."

"I'm hoping you and Molly will talk to the people on Russell's list and see what you get," Jesse said. "Molly will provide police authority. It's your case more than mine."

"Molly's smart," Sunny said.

"She is," Jesse said. "Best cop I got."

Sunny smiled.

"Don't tell Suit," she said.

"Suit's got potential," Jesse said.

"And what do we do about Cheryl?" Sunny said. "Now that her career at the Bond of the Renewal appears finished?"

"She's eighteen?" Jesse said.

"Yes."

"Can she stay with Spike?" Jesse said.

"For a while," Sunny said. "But then what?"

"Sink or swim?" Jesse said.

"Sooner or later," Sunny said. "But she's not ready for that yet."

"Some people are at eighteen," Jesse said.

"Some eighteen-year-olds are better trained," Sunny said.

"So, what do we do with her until she's trained?" Jesse said.

"Well, her parents continue to send her money," Sunny said.

"Under the threat of blackmail, I believe."

"Exactly," Sunny said. "So we know we can count on it."

"Fear is good," Jesse said.

"And what makes it so satisfying is that they did the wrong thing because they were so status-conscious," Sunny said.

"And you're now able to use that to make them do the right thing," Jesse said.

"Yes."

"Plus the fear of criminal prosecution," Jesse said.

"Plus that."

"But she can't simply live with Spike and subsist on her allowance," Sunny said.

"No."

"So, what do we do with her?" Sunny said.

" 'We'?" Jesse said.

"Of course 'we,' " Sunny said. "You're the chief of police."

"A heavy burden," Jesse said.

"And my special friend," Sunny said.

"Not so heavy a burden," Jesse said.

"So, what do we do?"

Jesse was quiet for a time.

Then he said, "I don't know."

"Me, either," Sunny said.

NEITHER HEALY NOR LIQUORI knew where Bob Davis was.

"He ain't even in the system," Healy said on the phone. "I know he's been with Reggie for a long time. But we got no record he's ever been arrested."

Jesse hung up and put his feet on his desk. A drink would be good. He was pleased with helping Sunny with the Bond of the Renewal. Whatever the disposition, the Bond was gone. The selectmen would be happy. Funny how he often felt more like drinking when he was happy than when he was sad. Maybe Sunny was right. Maybe he wasn't an alcoholic; maybe he just enjoyed drinking. *Except for the bender I went on over the Bang Bang Twins.* Maybe he was an alcoholic only when he was unhappy.

He smiled at himself and shook his head. *I only drink under two circumstances: when I'm happy and when I'm not.* Bob Davis had been with Reggie a long time. He was a bad guy, but he was a loyal guy. Ray Mulligan was the same way. And he'd been close enough to Davis for Davis to tell him about the twins' assault on his chastity.

Jesse took his feet down and let his chair tip forward. He looked at his desk calendar. Among the many things scribbled on there was Ray Mulligan's phone number. He found it and dialed.

When Mulligan answered he said, "Jesse Stone."

"Yeah?"

"You know where Bob Davis is?" Jesse said.

"Man, you don't fuck around," Mulligan said. "No 'Hey, how ya doin', Ray'? No 'How's it going'?"

"Do you?" Jesse said.

"Why would I know where Bob Davis is," Mulligan said.

"You're the same kind of guy, do the same kind of work," Jesse said. "And you were living next to each other for years."

There was silence for a time on Mulligan's end of the line.

Then he said, "If I knew where Bobby was, whaddya want?"

"I want to see him."

"Why?"

"I'm trying to nail down what happened to Knocko."

"Maybe I could come up with a phone number," Mulligan said.

"Works better in person," Jesse said.

"Yeah," Mulligan said.

"I got no hidden agenda here," Jesse said. "I'm not after him. To my knowledge, he's committed no crime."

Mulligan gave a short laugh.

"To my knowledge," Jesse said.

"Sure," Mulligan said.

Mulligan was silent for another moment.

"You're a stand-up guy," Mulligan said. "Your word: If I knew where he was and got him to meet you, he walks away from this meeting as free as he came."

"My word," Jesse said.

More silence.

Then Mulligan said, "I'll call you back."

64

SUITCASE SIMPSON WAS in the squad room with his feet up on the conference table, drinking coffee and reading the newspaper, when Jesse came in.

"Suit," Jesse said. "I want you to pick up Normie Salerno and bring him in and hold him for questioning."

"Guy that works for Reggie Galen?" Suit said.

"Yep."

"Big guy," Suit said. "Weight lifter."

"Take some guys," Jesse said. "Normie may not come peacefully."

"Where will you be?" Suit said.

"I'm the chief of police," Jesse said. "I try to remain above the fray."

Suit nodded.

"Especially when the fray is with an ape who may not come peacefully," he said.

"Don't be disrespectful to your chief," Jesse said.

"How long you think we can hold him?" Suit said. "Working for Reggie, he'll be lawyered up by the time we get him in here."

"Not if Reggie doesn't know we've got him," Jesse said.

"We follow him around until we get him alone?"

"He'll be spending the afternoon with a woman," Jesse said.

"How do you know that?" Suit said.

"Years of experience," Jesse said, "fighting crime."

"And," Suit said, "you're the chief of police."

"And," Jesse said, "she told me."

"Who's the woman?" Suit said.

"Name's Natalya," Jesse said.

"I don't know any Natalya," Suit said.

"That's right," Jesse said.

Jesse handed him a scrap of paper.

"Here's her address," Jesse said.

"We bring the woman in?"

"No," Jesse said.

"She know we're coming?" Suit said.

"Yes," Jesse said. "I talked with her this morning."

"There's stuff going on that I don't get," Suit said.

"There is," Jesse said. "Just go get him and hold him till I get back."

"Where you going?"

"Gotta talk to a guy," Jesse said.

"What guy?"

"Guy who might tell me things," Jesse said.

"I could go talk to the guy," Suit said. "And you could bring in the weight lifter. Be sure the job's done right."

Jesse smiled.

"I have every confidence in you, Suit," he said. "Just keep Normie here until I come back. No one sees him. No one knows he's here."

"What happens if somehow someone finds out and a lawyer shows up?" Suit said.

"Deceive him," Jesse said.

"Or her," Suit said.

"Or both," Jesse said.

65

JESSE MET BOB DAVIS sitting on a bench in a pavilion on Revere Beach. It was gray weather, overcast and spitting rain. The tide was high, and the dark waves foamed in close to the pavilion. The wind off the water was unseasonable, and the long beach was nearly empty except for a woman and a dog. The woman threw a ball. The dog chased it.

"Thanks for seeing me," Jesse said, when he sat down.

Davis nodded. He was wearing a tan raincoat with the collar up.

"Whaddya need?" Davis said.

"I want to know who killed Petrov Ognowski, and who killed Knocko."

"You wearing a wire?" Davis said.

"Nope."

"Mind if I pat you down?" Davis said.

"Nope."

Jesse stood, took his gun off his hip, held it in his right hand, and put both hands above his head.

"Pat," he said.

Davis went over him carefully. When he was through, Jesse put the gun back on his hip and sat back down.

"So, tell me about life on Paradise Neck," Jesse said.

"What I say here stays here," Davis said.

Jesse nodded.

"If you tell me you killed these people, you walk away clean," he said. "And tomorrow I start looking for you. Otherwise, you'll never see me again."

"I didn't kill them," Davis said. "And I ain't gonna help you nail Reggie. I was with him a long time; I owe him that."

Jesse nodded.

"Whaddya know?" Davis said.

"I don't know much for certain," Jesse said. "But I think Normie Salerno killed both of them."

Davis shrugged.

"He pulled the trigger," he said.

"And Normie killed Knocko."

"He pulled the trigger," Davis said. "On Knocko, too."

"Who told him to?" Jesse said.

Davis was looking at the dog chasing the ball.

"Nice-looking dog," he said.

"I'll take that to mean Reggie told him to," Jesse said.

"I like dogs," Davis said. "Never had a chance to own one."

"Why did Reggie tell him to do it?"

"What do you know about the twin wives," Davis said.

"Enough," Jesse said.

"They make a move on you?"

"Yep."

"They are some sick broads," Davis said.

"Yep."

"Well," Davis said. "Here's what I think went down. I didn't know it when it happened. I'm still not sure of all the details, but I'm in the ballpark."

Jesse nodded.

"They was playing their game with Petey," Davis said. "Petey was a good kid, but he was a moron. Instead of enjoying the ride, he decides he's made his fortune. He tries to blackmail the both of them."

"With what?" Jesse said.

"I don't know. I think he had evidence. Pictures, tape recordings, something. Easy enough to rig if he did a little planning."

"Easy," Jesse said. "So, he went to the women?"

"No," Davis said. "He went to Knocko and Reggie."

Jesse waited.

"And as I get it, Knocko was in a funk. He wants Petey dead. But he knows Petey is one of Reggie's people and he don't want to ace him without, like, clearing it."

"So he did and Reggie said he'd take care of it," Jesse said.

"What I figure," Davis said. "But Reggie never says nothing to me. I don't know why. He's embarrassed? He knows I kind of like Petey? Doesn't want to ask me to do one of our own, you know, somebody in the outfit?"

"You think he knew about the twins?" Jesse said.

"Yeah," Davis said. "He did. They was both playing house with him, same time they was playing house with Petey."

"Kind of dangerous," Jesse said.

"Maybe why they did it," Davis said.

"Probably," Jesse said.

"Stuff's too hard for me," Davis said. "So I don't know who killed Petey, and nobody else seems to know, and nobody seems much to give a shit, and . . . life goes on."

"How about Knocko," Jesse said.

"I guess Knocko gave a shit," Davis said. "I guess he was pretty mad about his wife doing a low-level thug like Petey."

"He didn't know about the Bang Bang Twins?" Jesse said.

"I don't think so," Davis said.

"He thinks she's been faithful," Jesse said.

Davis nodded.

"Poor slob," he said. "He can't get over it, and I guess he got to slapping his wife around."

"Because of her fling with Petey," Jesse said.

"Yep."

"And she spoke to her sister, and her sister spoke to Reggie. . . ."

Davis nodded.

"And Reggie says to me he wants Knocko whacked. And I

say, 'Whack Knocko? You been friends forever.' And Reggie says, 'He's been beating up my wife's sister. They both want him dead.' And I say, 'What about Ray?' And Reggie says, 'Don't worry about Ray. Ray's gone.' "

"The twins got him fired," Jesse said.

"Anyway, I'm saying, 'This is crazy. Just have her move out,' and Reggie's saying, 'You do it or I get somebody else to do it.' And I say, 'Who,' and he says, 'Normie.' And I say, 'Normie's a blow.' And Reggie says, 'Yeah, well, he done Petey okay.' "

"Easy enough if they think you're their friend," Jesse said.

"Is," Davis said. "Was. Both of them. The hard part for Normie would be shutting up about it afterwards."

"He didn't," Jesse said.

"Good," Davis said. "So he can take the fall."

"I'm going to try to take all of them down," Jesse said. "But I'll do it by flipping Normie. I won't use anything of yours."

Davis nodded.

"I told him," Davis said. "Those two broads are running your life, and it's gonna cause trouble. And he says, 'Bobby, I can't let you talk about my wife that way.' . . . I don't think the poor bastard knows by now which one his wife is . . . and I say, 'Reggie, you're thinking with your dick.' And he says, 'You're fired.' And I left."

They were silent, watching the woman and the dog. The dog was playing with the waves, chasing them as they rolled out, skittering away from them as they came in.

"So, why'd you tell me all this?" Jesse said.

"Normie pulled the trigger," Davis said. "And Reggie probably told him to do it. But it's those goddamned nymphos that are guilty."

"And you wanted me to know that," Jesse said.

"I guess so."

"What are you gonna do now?" Jesse said.

"Maybe get a couple dogs," Davis said.

66

JESSE SAT in his office with Nicolas Ognowski sitting hugely on a chair in the corner. Suit and Eddie Cox brought Normie into Jesse's office. There was a bloody-looking welt on one side of his forehead.

"Banged his head," Suit said, "when he was getting into the squad car."

"My lawyer's gonna hear about this," Normie said.

He eyed Ognowski, who was silent and motionless.

"Sit," Jesse said.

Suit steered Normie to the chair, and he sat. Suit went and leaned against the doorjamb.

"You need me, Jesse?" Cox said.

Jesse shook his head, and Cox disappeared.

"Who's this guy," Normie said, and nodded at Ognowski.

Jesse took a tape recorder out of his desk drawer and placed it on the desk in front of Normie.

"What's that for," Normie said. "You think I'm gonna make some kind of statement?"

Jesse pushed the play button and Natalya Ognowski's recording began to play. It took Normie a little time to realize what it was. When he did, he seemed paralyzed by it. The tape rolled on in all its remorseless banality.

"*I kill someone, two someones, right in town,*" he said.

"*In Paradise?*"

"*Absolutely,*" Normie said. "*You probably read about it in the papers.*"

"*The two men on Paradise Neck?*"

"*Bingo,*" Normie said.

"*I do not believe that,*" Natalya said.

"*Ognowski,*" Normie said, "*and Moynihan.*"

In the corner, Nicolas Ognowski made a sound like a sigh. Jesse held his hand up toward him. Normie seemed to get smaller in his chair.

"We gotcha, Normie," Jesse said.

"That lying bitch," he said.

"She's Petrov Ognowski's widow," Jesse said.

"Jesus," Normie said.

"And the large gentleman in the corner is Petrov Ognowski's father."

"What's he doing here?" Normie said.

"I have come," Nicolas said, "to look at the man who killed my son."

271

His voice sounded like it had rumbled up from hell.

"I see him again," Nicolas said, "I will know him."

"I was just following orders," Normie said.

"You can tell us about that, might help you a little," Jesse said.

"I can't snitch," Normie said.

"Why not?"

"They'll kill me?"

"Who?"

"You know what they do to snitches in jail," Normie said.

"You want to take the jump on this one yourself?" Jesse said.

"I just done what I was told," Normie said.

"Juries love that, killing two people because someone told you to. I'm guessing life, no parole."

Normie shook his head.

In a small voice, he said, "I want a lawyer."

Jesse glanced at Nicolas. Then looked back at Normie.

"You don't need one," Jesse said. "You're free to go."

"Huh?"

"You're free to go," Jesse said. "Beat it."

"You're not arresting me?"

"Nope," Jesse said. "Take a walk."

Normie stood up carefully, as if he'd been ill and was just recovering. In the corner, Nicolas Ognowski stood up. Normie glanced at him.

"What's he doing," Normie said.

"I guess he's leaving, too."

Normie took a step toward the door, and Nicolas moved

to follow. Normie stopped. He looked at Ognowski, then at Jesse.

"You're letting me and him go out together?"

"Sure," Jesse said.

"I . . . You can't do that."

"Sure I can," Jesse said.

"He . . . he's . . . For God's sake, man, I don't even have a piece."

"I'm not interested in fucking around with this," Jesse said. "You roll over on Reggie and the girls, in which case I keep you here. Or you refuse and stroll off into the sunset with Mr. Ognowski."

Ognowski was standing next to Normie now. He seemed to take up most of the room. Jesse could smell his sweat and whatever strong he'd had for lunch. Normie didn't look at him. Jesse wasn't sure, it might just have been breathing, but it sounded like a low growl might have come from deep in Ognowski's chest.

Normie turned away and came back to Jesse's desk and sat back down in the chair.

"Whaddya want to know," he said.

67

JESSE LAY against the propped pillows in Sunny's big cano-
pied bed. Sunny lay beside him. Jesse had a scotch and soda.
Sunny had a gimlet. Both of them were naked.

"We got Reggie cold, and Normie," Jesse said. "But the
ADA tells me she doesn't think she can make a case on the
Bang Bang Twins."

"Really?" Sunny said. "Accessories before or after?"

"They deny everything. And Reggie says they weren't
involved."

"Normie?" Sunny said.

"Everything he knows about their involvement is hearsay."

"How about their sex lives?"

"Adultery is rarely prosecuted these days," Jesse said.

"You call what they do adultery?" Sunny said. "That's like calling the Second World War assault."

"Reggie says they are innocent of all wrongdoing. He says Rebecca was a model wife, and Roberta a lovely sister-in-law."

"The ADA offer him any incentive to roll on them?" Sunny said.

"Yep," Jesse said. "But he won't."

"So, the Bang Bang Twins are free to, ah, ply their wares where they will," Sunny said.

"They are."

"Yet they very probably caused it all," Sunny said.

"Very probably," Jesse said.

"And they get off free," Sunny said.

"Well, Petrov Ognowski's father and widow know about them," Jesse said.

Sunny sipped her gimlet and looked at him over the rim.

"You told them," she said.

"I did," Jesse said.

"My God," she said.

"There's justice and maybe there's justice," Jesse said.

Sunny stared at him, then put the glass down and rolled over on top of him.

"You are absolutely frightening," she said. "Sometimes."

"And sometimes not," Jesse said.

He put his drink on the bedside table and put his arms around her.

Sunny kissed him.

When she stopped, Jesse said, "Didn't we just do this?"

"We did," Sunny said. "But I think you're man enough to do it again."

"Why do you think so?" Jesse said.

"I believe I have evidence," Sunny said.

"Maybe you should tamper with it," Jesse said.

They made love.

When they were done they lay, with Sunny's head on his chest, as their breathing settled.

After a while Sunny said, "That was a nice little interlude."

"It was," Jesse said. "Though I might object to the word *little*."

Sunny rubbed her face against his chest and giggled.

"Did you just giggle?" Jesse said.

"I did."

"You never giggle," he said.

"Now I do," Sunny said.

Jesse got up and made them two more drinks.

"You made any progress on what to do with Cheryl DeMarco?" he said, when he was back on the bed.

Sunny smiled.

"Spike says he's had sex with the dean of admissions at Hampton College," Sunny said.

"And feels that Cheryl could gain admission there?" Jesse said.

"He does."

"Well, that's some sort of solution," Jesse said.

"She'll live at the college, Spike says, and can visit on holidays or weekends or whatever."

"Is this a done deal?" Jesse said.

"No, but Spike has a date with this guy on Friday night, and he says he'll wrap it up then."

"Must be an interesting experience," Jesse said. "Dating Spike."

"Something neither you nor I will ever know," Sunny said.

She drank from her new gimlet.

"I have, I believe, boffed your socks off twice this evening," Sunny said. "And I want to know what you and Dix talked about."

"In regard to the Bang Bang Twins?"

"Yes."

Jesse took a deep breath and let it out, and told her.

"Wow," Sunny said, when he was through. "Aren't we a pair?"

"You need to avoid control; I need to control."

"Something of a mismatch," Sunny said.

Jesse nodded.

"Still, we seem to get along," Sunny said.

"And maybe we can change our needs," Jesse said.

"Maybe," Sunny said.

"Maybe we love each other," Jesse said.

"Maybe," Sunny said.

"Maybe we should proceed on the assumption that we do," Jesse said, "and see what develops."

"I agree," Sunny said.

Jesse put his hand up. Sunny gave him a high five.

"What's the next step?" Jesse said.

"I think we should order in some Chinese food," Sunny said.

"What an auspicious start," Jesse said.